Published by Semiotext(e)
PO BOX 629, South Pasadena, CA 91031
www.semiotexte.com

Cover: Hervé Guibert, *Sans titre*, 1980. Silver gelatin print 18 x 12 inches. Courtesy of Hervé Guibert Estate, Paris, and Callicoon Fine Arts, New York

Design: Hedi El Kholti
ISBN: 978-1-63590-132-0

Distributed by the MIT Press, Cambridge, MA, and London, England. Printed and bound in the United States of America.

10   9   8   7   6   5   4   3   2

Stephanie LaCava

The Superrationals

semiotext(e)

Contents

Like my mother had once been, I was manic, hyper-aware of the world, but without the same mooring.

Half her life was spent naive and wide-open. By the time she had me at twenty-four, she had pivoted to careful withholding. So sure of her place, she was able to shape shift into characters, sound and affect. The ritual of editing, crossing out, penciling in, was hypnotic for her, certain. At thirty-eight, she met the writer Robert Northwell and they would work together for the rest of her life. Five more years.

My mother looked almost identical to me when she was my age. People who knew her tell me this all the time. Where this begins, I am still unformed, in my twenties, still thinking that at any moment my body could be replaced by that of another, still waiting to be flooded with validation. Late to my mother's schedule. By my age, she was led by something completely different, a strange mechanism, phantom calm. It never occurred to her that she wouldn't be okay.

I was seventeen when she died. My father passed away a year later, but we hadn't seen one another in a long time. I met Jack when I moved to New York to go to university. This relationship became the sole grounding force in my life, a hard phenomenon to explain to someone who has never felt this flimsy, this disposable. A false step, and I would become someone else entirely, as if the years leading up to the present were lost.

Unplugged. Unmoored. Without backstory.

(I should probably mention Gretchen too.)

Robert Norton

I write at the same time every day. Sit down at my desk, survey the piles, and write. It has been years since I have been able to see the color of the metal beneath all my papers. I never ask the girl to clean it. I tell her not to. But she takes it upon herself to do so. She wants to impress me. When I first interviewed her, she said, "I crimson all your books."

I was disappointed to not have realized sooner that she had substituted "crimson" for "red," and meant "read." Olympia would have loved this. The girl's English, a second language: color homonym as the blankness of seeing in written word.

I liked the young cleaner girl after this, the way you like someone who reminds you even indirectly of someone else. She wore a funny thick black Mepris-style headband with tie-dye shirts and cut-off jeans. Earlier that day, she had rearranged my papers into neat stacks, a large grid separated by depressed lines of gray. All my cigarettes had been thrown into the yellowing filing cabinet. I found them not because I was looking for them, but because I was looking for my box wherein I kept all my special letters. It is an old thing, but so am I.

Under the loose cigarettes was a mound of ancient stationery that Olympia had bought me. Ribboned stacks of off-white cards trimmed in fine navy blue line. The stock exposed to light had turned beige. Most of the notes had been signed by me long ago, to be tossed into books I sent out.

I often think of her, how she would steal the cards for herself and write lists, leaving them behind for me to find. This had been most disconcerting after her death. It's continued for ten years. I still discover them from time to time, her hand, that tiny script. We never once emailed. Only post. Or fax. I told you, I am an old thing.

Nearly seventy. It took me that long to finally do something aside from my art.

Last year, I established a residency here at the house. It was never intended to be explicitly for American writers, but we received so many applicants from those MFA programs. It had been a brutal slog. Writers always want other writers to read their stuff, but then they cannot make anything good of their own. That is why I loved Olympia, aside from the obvious. She was the first person to read my work. My preferred editor. We had a lot of misunderstandings, but none because of my writing.

It occurred to me that morning that the girl may have misplaced an important document and so I fumbled through a few piles looking for it. The search became more frantic as I dug into the bottom drawer, veiny blue mole hands. Nothing. I pushed aside one pile, knocked over another.

To the near right of my desk was a tumbling stack of the third reprint of the least favorite of my books. I was supposed to sign them to send back to a few shops. In this day, authors often do that when they pass by or make an appearance. I do neither: no passing by and no appearances. I work. Sometimes when they send these boxes, I sign them, but hide my signature. Then, the bookstore employees have to find it. They always call asking why I sent the box back.

Olympia said all the best men were half trickster. Makes me smile.

That morning, I sat at my desk for longer than usual without working. While looking for the envelope, I'd found a neat stack of photographs turned face down, the Kodak stock bleeding into the messy columns. I picked the pile up and flicked through it, each rectangle, orange date seared at the bottom, the digits in neon bars like those of an electric clock. It had been a long time since I'd seen any of them. A big green palm frond from some botanical garden; a round thing reflected in a big vitrine; Olympia and her daughter staring back at me, two pairs of pretty eyes. I turned them over, faces down. There would be someone else in the house soon and I didn't want anything personal left lying about.

The writer I had selected to start the program was to arrive soon. His winning application had been a strange thing. No one else on the committee had agreed, but I convinced them. One had said he reminded her of a young version of myself. I'm not sure.

His name was Christopher Swan, he had gotten his MFA from Iowa, which had annoyed me when I found out, but by then it was too late. I'd already fallen for the story.

"Acconci went to Iowa," Olympia once said mockingly.

"Dropped out," I replied.

"When he read Mallarme," she said on cue and rolled her eyes.

I didn't want some young guy to live with me for two months, but he was on his way. I admired his work. It had a kind of taste. Perhaps taste was the wrong word, a sensibility. It wasn't fully realized, but it was there, an intangible abstract thing.

But honestly, I would really prefer just to be alone.

PART I:
UNPLUGGED IN NEW YORK

September 2015, New York

Weird how you can know all kinds of second hand things about a woman and not know what her voice sounds like. Just the sound of those other women talking about her.

It was always other women who contributed to these expository narratives.

I first heard about Mathilde because of things girls had said to me. They'd brought her up. How I needed to avoid her. To stay away.

I first saw her with that guy. Her husband? They said she was funny-looking, like an alien creature. She was beautiful with thick brown hair, green eyes and built like a dancer, but didn't move like one.

That night, it was clear to me from her half empty stare, she was holding it together to be sure no one could get in and wedge open the cracks.

They were all over her, though.

Her slouched posture, her foot that kept tapping the floor, as if it was going to walk away without her. That guy kept his hand on her shoulder. It seemed like the only thing keeping her there, in the room, on the planet.

I had wanted to talk to her, but she only met my look and then, angled away. She wasn't looking around to see who was looking at her or who else she should try and talk to. Instead, she was looking for an exit strategy, like she couldn't bear it one more minute.

I'd heard their stories. But again, I'd never heard her talk.

We had decided we didn't like Mathilde even before we met her. In our sisterhood, objective reality played no part, it was easy to dislike someone we knew so little about. We made up her mythology, just as we had our own.

When Charles came into the office, we always pretended we were all cool, assumed neutral poses and careful silence.

Some days he slipped past us to show us he was there, walked by without even looking our way, wanted us to know he was watching.

That day, after he was gone, Alice let out a laugh and we were alive again.

"Do you know what she wrote her dissertation about?"

"Who cares."

"No, really. You have to hear this."

"It was something about beauty and betrayal, and objects, based off that Mike Kelley show that was at the Tate. Something strange with body parts and dead saints, disembodiment—or dismemberment?"

"There's a rumor that she's thinking about going back for her PhD."

"She's so entitled."

"Speaking of entitled, can we talk for a minute about Will? I'm so tired of these up and coming artists talking big moral game. Then, they're bank-rolled by their 'daughter-of girlfriend.'"

"But his girlfriend's mother is an artist, a legitimate one."

"Who are you talking about?"

"Dating the kid of a talented person doesn't make you one by transference."

"You mean osmosis."

"Social capital counts."

We nodded.

"Mathilde's husband doesn't work in the art world."

"Correct."

"Why do you think she married him?"

"He's really nerdy."

"Why would she go back to school?"

"She already has a husband."

"Her best friend's that terrible, odd girl who sleeps with Sam."

"I thought she was straight? She had an affair with Christopher?"

"You know she doesn't use her real last name."

"What do you mean?"

"She's from some family, but uses her middle name: Gretchen Salt."

"Salt was her middle name?"

"Why doesn't she use her real name, would probably help her cause."

"Her cause is different than yours."

"I think it's clear her lack of cleverness."

We didn't argue. We didn't really know what half that meant.

"Were you in class with her at all?"

"She's younger than us. We'd all graduated by the time she arrived."

"How did she get into Contemporary?"

"Doll parts."

"So where exactly is she now?"

"The library or wherever it is she goes."

"I thought she was away, traveling somewhere with Jack."

"Jack?"

"Yes, that's her husband."

"Have you ever seen him?"

"Once. He was wearing a navy blue sweater and funny old man running shoes."

"Hot enough."

"She's super weird." Charles was coming back. We lined up our chairs and faced our computers.

There are four of us in the department, and Mathilde. She joined as a junior specialist not too long ago. Charles is the head of contemporary, renowned for his management skills and taste. The pressing challenge: to procure works from uncooperative artists and collectors while identifying new talent, and managing entitlement at the office, studio and among clients.

For a while, Charles had his eyes set on one young painter: a thirty-four-year-old artist named Tom Belier.

Tom was evasive, always between two spaces, one in Paris—his dirty, perpetually rented hotel room somewhere in the 6eme arrondissement—or his downtown studio space, where he worked but also slept. It was not meant to seem glamorous. Rumors were that the New York space had come from discrete, humble collectors, an early real estate acquisition that remained rent controlled. They were the same couple of the '80s urban legend that placed one half of a then unknown "graffiti artist" living on their couch.

"False alarm," someone group texted. Charles had bypassed the office.

We went back to our zig zag of chairs, arranged so that we could see one another.

"Why is it that Mathilde's the only one of us Tom will talk to?"

"Because she's weird."

"That's appealing?"

"She's beautiful?"

"I think he likes that she's the odd one in this."

"Odd is correct."

And, as usual, the conversation started to sound the same. We were loyal to mutual hate.

"So fucking cool and Bohemian."

"She's married."

"Super annoying that Charles let her go away this week on diplomatic wife duty."

"There's so much to do."

"But really, I wonder why Mathilde's the only one he'll talk to?"

"I don't like her."

"None of us do."

"She shouldn't have taken off like that when she was starting to prove herself."

"Remember when she'd just graduated from the Courtauld, claimed she'd had an internship at The National Gallery."

"That was like eight years ago now."

"No one has an internship at the National Gallery."

"Seriously."

"Where did she go for uni?"

"Uni? Are you English all of a sudden?"

"Oxford, I think. Or Maybe Brown. No, Columbia. I heard she had very little money to get through school, some issue with a complicated family. She pretends like she worked so hard, slogging time as a research assistant and odd hours servicing the antiquarian book dealer."

Collective laughter at the emphasis on servicing.

"And now she lives in an old townhouse in the '90s. It's quite lovely."

"I thought she lived in a loft?"

"I bet Oxford's where she met that husband. Honeytrap kind of thing."

"He went to Cambridge."

"Like Harvard?"

"Charles hired her because he thinks she's hot."

"She doesn't even have a position, really. It's some kind of hybrid client artist relations thing, which sounds like bullshit to me."

"Everyone's everything nowadays."

"Her name's French. Is she even French? That's kind of pretentious."

For Halloween a few days ago, we'd dressed up as a Baldessari, worn white, red and blue circle masks with tiny cut-outs at the eyes. Someone's housekeeper had made them from foam core and felt.

A framed black and white picture of us was now on the department desk, the silver frame, a gift from Alice's mother. Mathilde had been excluded from the group: an aesthetic decision. (We always included her in our gossip.) There was some paperwork and a few phone calls to be finished before we were picked up by car to go home and repeat the same routine the following day.

Mathilde de Saint-Evans

February 2007, New York

Gretchen listened for hours to the details of my last breakup, patient as I asked over and over what she thought went wrong. Usually by the time we passed the twenty minute mark, she would light a joint, but she always stayed long after the drugs were gone.

"You have to accept that he's gone. He's not coming back." She waited a beat to seem less self-involved. "Can I show you a letter that I wrote to Christopher?"

"Okay, but he's treated you like garbage. You two haven't slept together in months and still this psychodrama."

> *Dear Christopher,*
> *I love you because of your argument for your art—*
> *and in spite of it. You tell me that all these high*
> *rolling men and their numbers and charts are one day*
> *away from disaster. And that stories are a commodity*
> *that man has never, will never, be able to live with-*
> *out. It's an honest living, becoming more difficult to*
> *execute in an honest fashion.*
> *I must remind you:*
> *There are wars being fought over resources, like coal or*
> *oil. You can't clothe or feed a nation with stories.*
> *Love, Gretchen*

I burst out laughing.

"That's fucked up," Gretchen said.

"It's hilarious.

"I think he'll think it's brilliant."

"I don't know…"

"Mathilde, come on. You're not a writer. You don't know."

"It's unclear whether Christopher is one either."

"Just because your mother was some legendary editor, you think you know about writers, words."

"That's not it."

"In fairness, you do plan on doing the same thing: spend your life working with old white men, obsessed with mark making."

"I don't know what I want to spend my life doing."

"The good news is it won't be Jonathan."

"That's callous." A few hours earlier, I'd received a call from the woman who lived next to the house where I grew up outside the city. She'd seen a man drop a garbage bag on the doorstep. I asked her if she would mind checking its contents. She'd phoned me back and listed a number of pieces of clothing, a stuffed donkey, books, a laptop, a Discman and an old pack of birth control. Everything I'd left behind at my ex Jonathan's place.

"Imagine this," Gretchen started, trying to make me laugh. "Jonathan sitting in his house in Greenwich in a few years. His wife is wearing bubblegum pearl earrings. He's reminiscing about his glory days playing lacrosse and listening to Jay Z and Cypress Hill. He calls you up, but you don't answer because you're busy and have an awesome life. He leaves a message. 'Sorry for leaving your stuff at your door.'"

"Funny."

"You know he did it to maximize his eventual pay off. You were too free-spirited, too much of a wild card to continue to invest. He had to get out before you did."

"You and your behavioral economics."

"*You* and your tendency to be unreasonable most of the time."

It was all part of another of the frequent, strangely mature, comedic lectures Gretchen liked to deliver. She majored in philosophy, thought maybe she'd be a philosopher and devote her inheritance to spread awareness of other philosophers. This plan was short lived, when she decided to drop out, but not before she'd bulldozed through her share of thinkers and assorted acolytes. Psychoanalysis was her latest obsession. She had a photographic memory and could read three books in one evening. As a teenager, boarding school had been too easy for her. Instead of going to class, she would stay in her room and make art; until coke got in the way.

I, on the other hand, was too careful, had always been, worried I was destined for an accident, an explosion, a misstep. The problem with keeping straight when you're young is you inevitably need to fill that void of experience. It's only a matter of when.

An unstable new friendship with Gretchen was the slightly better alternative to the uppity girls' savage bids to stay alive and ahead of one another. I had a keen sense of a strange undercurrent among all of them. That it was better to betray one another than cooperate for anything other than appearances. I felt safe with Gretchen. She had free days and nights free and I liked staying in. And she was smart, and fun.

"I have some new ideas."

"You have ideas!?"

"Fuck off. But, listen, first."

"Go ahead."

"I think I've identified your problem. You have—we all have—images that loop and rattle around, lurk until summoned by randomness, an object or person of eerie recognition, same original lines and shapes. What you call taste or aesthetics." (Here she rolled her eyes.) "It's a Frankenstein of feelings activated by one of these things. You don't match 1 to 1, you can't even begin to know what 1 is, except that you want to, you desire it, to feel something like pleasure in its sameness."

"Write that down!" I teased her and started laughing.

"Watch this space, Mathilde."

"What space?"

"The sticky, unadorned walls of your body, organs, arteries, sneaky aneurysms. Pay attention to unease. This is ground control before the untamed migrates to your head."

"What does this have to do with my broken heart?"

"That's disappointing. Your broken heart? Human hearts heal quick, the empty lot behind the eyes is what takes time. Those who are depressed stay in the observation stage much longer, 'reverberant doubt.'"

"Did you smoke a little too much…"

"Don't be flippant. Jonathan's offered you a breakthrough, hard-to-see-now parting gift of *all your shit*, like literally all your shit. Instead of ruminating, walk away. Or at least get in bed with it, exorcise it. Don't look so disturbed. Trust me."

"Gretchen's greatest life hacks: The subconscious is a life hack."

"Slow down."

"Let's make a chart. Pin up all the evidence here." Gretchen gestured to the dorm wall covered in ant-size holes from tacks used to hang up clippings and papers. The entire wall was covered in porous cork, a kind of padded room-cum-life-size mood board.

The top of the square was already covered in clippings of Gretchen from fashion and celebrity magazines. She'd used people's disproportionate interest in her style and family to see how far she could push it. ("I've never done anything worth an editorial," she said to me.)

The top row was an editorial headlined, "The activist of her generation." She looked beautiful and hot and saleable. The caption didn't mention that she was planning a Philosopher Appreciation Organization. She said no one ever asked what her art or resistance was about, only what size she wore and if she'd be willing to cut her hair:

Zero and No.

Gretchen planned to recontextualize these tear sheets, it made her feel like a secret agent, like a spy with a messy agenda. I argued with her that she could be volunteering, at least getting in on the ground. "All the artists I admire upend systems, they are disruptive and playful."

"You are disruptive."

"Only a matter of time before it all shakes itself out. Your radical art history goddesses didn't get what they deserved until they were 70."

"The work didn't change. People were no longer distracted by their pretty, living, breathing bodies."

Gretchen tore out a page of a recent Berlin-based art magazine and tacked it to the top right on the wall. She was dressed in a neon yellow Giant Slalom Olympic suit type onesie. Instead, she was sitting down at a McDonalds eating a hamburger rolling her eyes into the back of her head. She drew a thick line with a Sharpie marker underneath.

"Here, I want you to pin up images that strike you, that you find pleasing. Only photos of these things, flat scaled down versions."

"Seems weird."

"Good, you're in."

"Why do you keep flickering your eyes like that? Are you going to cry?"

"Always happens when I come up with a great trick to efficiently clock our bleak existence. It's the apotheosis! Fear it!"

"You started using that word after you met Christopher. He uses that word a lot in his work."

"How do you know?"

"I started reading it when you started having meltdowns about him. Seemed the best place to look for evidence, because you ask me the most absurd questions about him that I would only be able to answer if I were psychic."

"What do you mean?" Her eyes settled and she sat down.

"Like, I have no idea whether or not he will call you tomorrow. I really want to give you an educated answer." With her financial security, Gretchen was fine to chase the great passion, over and over again.

"I thought you might try the Delusion Excuse."

"Spelled D-e-l-e-u-z-i-a-n."

"No, nice try."

"It's when you reason that someone, say Jonathan as example, wasn't in touch not because he didn't want you, but because of a deficit on *his* part. So easy to say, 'You intimidate him' or 'he's worried about falling in love.'

This is not to say that he wasn't abusive, only to realize that within his own set of terms it was all rational. So, rarely does a man who really wants anything run the other way."

"Least effective way to spin that one."

"If by effective you mean to further the nonsense you tell yourself. Why not transfer that finite amount of energy to acknowledge he wasn't a match for you. Not some ridiculous algebraic mess to end up on top. What a waste of time. That's called ego."

"Whatever. You know I don't do that."

"I know, that's why you're my only friend. I don't need a bunch of sycophants borrowing my clothes."

"You're ridiculous."

"You know as well as I do that desire is not about the superlative nature of the object. Can we talk about those John-von-Neumann-Neuroses?"

"Can you try to be normal? And not name drop Neumann and Morgenstern."

"Both are so much more relevant to your love life than you can even begin to imagine."

"Just like your Kierkegaard-Seducer-Syndrome."

"I give all the diagnoses male names for good reason, and appropriate homage. Maybe first names would be better, Soren says that a very smart man believes himself to be doing a woman a favor by giving her sex and attention, that he's a pleasure seeker, driven by the chase. The end goal is not partnership, neither artistic nor domestic. (Unless the latter involves a kind of Vera Nabokovian sacrifice). Soren stalks the unwitting woman acutely aware where weakness shows an opening. There needs to be an element of feeling chosen, that the on-looker sees something different from everyone else and if he goes that too will disappear."

"You're trying to distract me from the real issue. When did you and Christopher start talking again? Three weeks ago you told him not to email, text or call you."

"Yeah, I've told him that a few times. He doesn't seem to care, especially not when he finds out I'm dating someone else. He knows about Sam."

"How do you know that?"

"He asked her. They ran into each other at some event. Sam came home and told me."

"She's aware of your past with Christopher?"

When Gretchen met Christopher he had been married and she had been working on a novel, looking for a *reader*. He obliged, and then claimed to be reading it for the next few weeks. But Gretchen had never pushed send on the email containing the attachment.

Until then, Gretchen had let her honey blonde hair go wild, long natural waves which she'd twist together and rarely brush. After meeting Christopher, she dyed her hair black and wore a single, tiny earring in her right ear for nine months, until she decided it hadn't really changed anything. So, she went back to blonde and looking exactly like her mother. Gretchen was a complicated kind of survivor. One could argue she made poor choices in service of personal mythology, but she just didn't think that hard about anything.

Christopher had been proud of her, until he was ashamed of her. She was ten years younger than him with tiny, pert breasts and an ass unlikely for someone so slight.

And she wasn't stupid or boring. They fucked every day for a year, always once after he had his coffee, right before he sat down to work. Gretchen declared one day that she was done with Christopher, and writing. It was suspect if he being done with her had come first.

"Sam made me tell her everything."

"You two are so Nathalie Barney and Djuna Barnes. And, as can be expected, Christopher is about to assert his pathetic self. Cue you telling me that he's been in touch."

"Exactly."

"You're unavailable. That's why."

"Beside the point," Gretchen dismissed it.

"Actually, more to the point. It's an example of your KSS. No lies were told. No promises made, even though he'd communicated without words all the while. He gives words too much power. The action is irrelevant."

"He'd tell you his genius is in that his words are ecstatic, like a painter, they happen and he puts them down, action-writing."

"It's called automatic writing."

"Exactly, full circle."

"How many women do you think he has in rotation at once?"

"Would be funny to put them all in a room, a few rooms."

"One problem is that they all speak different languages."

"I don't think that really matters."

"True."

"Code."

"It's already code."

"I'm going to create German, French, Latin, Greek hybrids."

"Very good use of time."

"'*der Vorhaltung,*' a suspension of a relationship to try out another candidate, only to return to the first if the impulse proves a short-sighted decision."

"And if that's misunderstood in translation, between lovers, it could mean the dissolution of all three connections."

"There's an in-between where it's as if one doesn't exist at all in the same plane."

"That's real time."

"Remember that photographer? He still texts you?"

I met Jack when I was twenty. I had been surprised when he told me he was American, and he had been surprised when I said the same of myself. He was twenty-nine when he first saw me, but thirty-one when we first spoke. Par for all his movements. Slow and careful. He had noticed my long wavy dark brown hair, green eyes, and awkwardness, unlike any of the girls he'd met in his classes, he said. He was working towards his doctorate at Columbia, the School of International and Public Affairs (SIPA) and I was an undergraduate in Arts and Sciences.

I remember seeing him, stoic, maybe just shy, everyone around him a little deferential. His brown curly hair needed to be cut and his sneakers were always undone. Still, he was the one who would, in time, feel protective of me.

When I first arrived in the city, I had been befriended by an older girl named Kate. She had brought me cookies and flowers and watched and listened as I cried prostrate on the dorm room floor post breakup. I had delayed going back to school as long as I could, following Jonathan on his trips for work. Kate liked to hear stories about the hotels and dinners, not least of all my deteriorating relationship. She asked me one day, "I heard your father is the head of sales at that house based in Vienna. Do you think you could help me get an internship?"

"My parents are dead," I had said.

When you're young and new to New York it can get lost that people are looking for friends who are *interesting*. The pursuit and capture of these intrigues probably shouldn't be called "friendships," but then the player would be given up before she or he had even started. Gretchen referred to them as *Vasodenemie* when I first met her. It took me a few weeks to realize this was the phonetic spelling of the French for enemy ships.

Back then, I had thought Jonathan was going through a moment and would, in time, respond to my calls and messages as one would after two years of partnership. I had the tendency to believe in someone as I had believed in Kate with whom I shared Jonathan's departure.

Two years later, and Kate could be found working as a gallerist in Paris. With her secured ambitions had gone any affection for me.

Eight years later, and still no word from Jonathan.

When I'd met Jonathan, he'd been quickly smitten, asking me to move in eight weeks later. He told me he'd take half of my pain and three years later all he'd taken was half of my adult life, and left without explaining why. He'd come in just as fast. I can still see his face when he was humiliating me. Weird that that is the only expression I can really remember. We had sex nearly every day when we were geographically together, but I rarely came. He forbade me to masturbate, because we had each other. It was the closest I'd ever felt in a relationship—eclipsed.

Jonathan never liked Gretchen. She had cautioned me against him, feeling his own distaste for her. I sometimes wondered where this circle started. It was as if he knew she would reject him and see his faults, mirror them off to me, because I wasn't able to see them clearly on my own. So, he set about boxing me off from the outside world.

A year in, he had insisted on taking me away for a surprise trip. First Barcelona where there had been a man along Las Ramblas with a drugged pet pug dressed as a clown who had yelled out to me in Catalan, "Beware."

And then we were on the train and in Bruges. The first morning, we fucked a few more times and then ate mussels for breakfast, which was mildly disgusting, but the local delicacy. They'd arrived in a big red iron pot, hard little open mouths sizzling. We laughed about it and fucked again and Jonathan pulled my hair until it hurt, and asked me to move in with him. From that moment forward I couldn't eat shellfish. "I'm not sure," I said. And he looked back at me like I had thrown his plate against the wall. Later, he pulled my hair harder. And so I admitted to feeling some combination of oxytocin and appreciation limited by an instinct to worry and lack of time to trust. "But I love you."

When we arrived in Paris, I had to take a few meetings for prospective internships and leave Jonathan behind at the hotel. I came back one afternoon and noticed that he'd removed his passport from the safe. And how it had been odd that the bellman had asked if I was fine as I climbed the stairs. That night, we fucked, but unlike days before. Jonathan came from behind hard and fast and wouldn't look at me. He then dressed quickly, even though there was nowhere to go but to sleep. I started to cry.

"Why are you crying?" he asked flippantly.

"You seem so cold, like all of a sudden I'm a girl you just picked up on the street," I said. "Why isn't your passport in the safe?"

"It is," he lied. "Are you crazy?"

"Why are you being so curt?"

"Mathilde, stop acting up."

"I thought you were concerned that I'm upset."

"You're being a crazy person."

"You said you'd be here this morning when I got back and you were out?"

"I never said that. I had to run an errand."

"Where did you go?"

"Just out for a run."

I continued to cry. Seeing this, Jonathan flipped me over and took off my skirt. I lifted off my jumper and started to pull off his shorts. He smelt of having gone for a run and I felt comforted by this familiar scent, and then, all the chemical others.

The next morning, I got up and went into the bathroom, trying not to wake him. I found his baseball cap to the side of the sink and threw it behind me onto the floor. It was odd that at his age, he still insisted on wearing a hat like that. It fit with his interest in creating heritage for himself by romantic association. He was also prematurely balding.

When we first met, I had been wearing a hat from a sailing outfitter. He'd approached me asking about it. The girlfriends before me had assorted hobbies that fit this framework, mostly equestrians. Jonathan liked to use the word "lifestyle." I hated him objectively, but no one had ever been so in.

I saw my eyes in the mirror, swollen and glassy. I splashed water on my face and put on my glasses. He was awake when I walked out.

"Why are you wearing your glasses?"

"My eyes are swollen."

"Yes, because you were a crazy person last night. I had to fuck you to calm you down."

"Sorry?"

He started to laugh. "C'mere." I could feel my eyes welling up again. "Seriously?" he said. Months earlier, I'd been inundated by earnest texts from him: "If You are Sad. I Will Take Half."

"Seriously. Mathilde. C'mere and stop acting up." There was a knock at the door as the coffees arrived. Jonathan had called for them when I was in the bathroom. I opened the door and he motioned the woman dressed in black to his side of the bed. I offered to relieve her of the silver tray. "No, put it here," he said taking the tray and placing it on the bed. "Thanks."

He picked up the espresso, added two sugars and handed it to me. After, I took the cup and saucer, he switched my hands so that I held the tiny handle with my left instead of my right. He nodded his head. The woman left the room. I took a sip. He grabbed the cup from me and it spilled all over the floor.

Three weeks later, I received the call that my belongings had been left on my parents' doorstep.

early draft / work in progress…

All art criticism throughout this book is strictly under copyright of Mathilde de Saint-Evans

Transmuting Desire: Memory, Mannequins, and The Contemporary Reliquary An Exploration of the Unsaid, Unseen, Uncanny, Space, the In Between

"I think the point where language breaks down as a useful tool of communication is the edge where poetry and art occurs." Bruce Nauman

"I am going to construct an artificial girl with anatomical possibilities which are capable of recreating the heights of passion, even of inventing new desires…The body is like a sentence that invites us to rearrange it, so that its real meaning becomes clear through a series of endless anagrams.

"What is at stake here is a totally new unity of form, meaning and feeling: language-images that cannot simply be thought up or written up." Hans Bellmer

In Mike Kelley's essay, "Playing with Dead Things," he writes of the art experience, as an encounter with an object "tied to an act of remembering." This essay accompanies his first staging of The Uncanny Show at Sonsbeek 93. The exhibition takes its title from the term used in Sigmund Freud's 1919 essay of the same name. It is a sensation of something that is strangely familiar, unsettling. There is arguably a rejection of the thing based on this feeling, but also an attraction, a draw to understand, categorize and dominate the passing instinct.

In this early essay, Kelley talks about how he collected images of figurative sculpture that embodied the uncanny feeling he sought to replicate in his show. The problem with these photographs was that they

were never to scale, everything shrunk down to fit 3 x 5 or so. Still, somehow the picture provoked an unconscious sensation in the onlooker. I will argue for the power of what is absent in a work of art, the uncanny effect of the space in between an object and its intended effect on the viewer. In writing, this is white space on the page or "space" between that which is plainly stated, frank, and its various elliptical interpretations in the reader. In both instances, that which is empty can be filled with projected narrative. As Bataille explains, human eroticism is different than animal sexuality, because it is fed by inner life and imagining.

From a political point of view, this would mean a fascist suppression of desires, with rules and control. Revolutionary poetics, forms, and practices to ignite the unconscious as practiced by the avant grade in times of protest. I wonder if this will get worse before it gets better with half of existence playing out in virtual space, making it even harder to pin down. The presence of the uncanny in artwork will only increase in the future, as religious fetishism of objects like icons or relics transmutes into the desire for a spatial thing to hold emotional and spiritual power which reconnects the viewer to primal feelings.

Works of art that can be referenced include, Mike Kelley's work (The Uncanny curation and Arenas); Greek letters or names in Cy Twombly's paintings

(Text & Misspellings); and a cross section of Marcel Broodthaer's oeuvre (Poetry & Decor.) This extends to happenings or actions like those of Carolee Schneemann or Cosey Fanni Tutti to create temporary situations which access the unconscious.

* * *

Still February 2007, New York

Back then, the first question for me when deciding on someone was to preemptively forget the eerie recognition of like between two people. My interactions were manufactured, a little fear-based, a little about the challenge, always with intention, because I hadn't been socialized to seek out my kind, but rather to please. It wasn't all that far off from Kate's approach. I see this now. My agenda was to stay on course; not to climb, but to avoid going backward, spiraling back to where I'd started from. I didn't want to lose any sort of control.

Gretchen could be calculated, but she played among her own kind, was drawn to them, despite her best efforts. She went through her days trying to derail her life and privilege, never quite succeeding. When we first met, I wasn't able to pinpoint what attracted me to her. In many ways, even our initial dynamic held uncanny similarities to that of me and my late mother.

I think, it was the surety of her disregard.

I wanted a relationship with Gretchen because of how it made me feel about myself.

After Kate had shed me, Gretchen and I would spend nights together at a local bar. On one of these evenings, Jack had been out late at the table next to us, sitting with a dark-eyed girl.

It was nearing three a.m. "Gretchen, we have to go," I urged her to leave.

"I'm fine. Go ahead without me." I didn't want to leave out of principle, but knew she wouldn't have it any other way, and I was exhausted from the day. It had been taxing, which was logically unreasonable. I hated it when Gretchen complained about her own exhaustion, because it was usually from nights of partying. I had become a kind of runaway without emotional or financial support. Gretchen was also a runaway, but from emotional and financial support. I felt protective of her for other reasons.

Frustrated by her insistence on staying that night, I left and wandered slowly the long way back to my dorm. Jack lapped me. We exchanged a look and then carried on.

He turned around and called out, "Was that you earlier?"

I pivoted and walked to meet him. "Yes."

"I'm Jack," he offered his hand.

I ignored it. "Mathilde."

He laughed and put down his hand. "Are you French?"

"No, my mother thought she was."

"I don't often—well, I actually never have—done this, but would you like to have dinner with me?"

I paused and looked at him standing disheveled in the street.

"Yes."

"Can I get your phone number?"

"Sure, 917…" I started.

"I'll call you," he said. I liked him immediately. He seemed certain of himself in a way I hadn't much encountered in boys of my own age.

The day after, Jack called to ask me to join him for dinner.

We met two nights later at a restaurant not far from the spot where I had first seen him. He showed up in the same corduroys, sneakers and a blue blazer as the only indication of effort. He was gentle when discussing his background, careful, it seemed, not to say too much or give anything away. He didn't need me, didn't need to make me want him.

That night, I decided I wanted him, because he didn't seem like he really wanted me. Eight years later, I wasn't sure I wanted him. His fault being that he was always there.

There had been a photographer I met at dinner two years earlier and just before that the collector. And after both of them, there had been the hockey player who wanted to be a painter and the banker wanted to be a hockey player. And just after Jonathan, there was Jack.

There were only a few people who made me lose the cloudiness, my foggy cover. I tested them too.

My mother told me that sometimes people take leave because of something you do, but there are actually two ways to rationalize deserting someone.

One is the hard-won legitimate step back. The other is more common: when someone finds the fail they'd been waiting for when you couldn't give them what they wanted. And what they wanted was you as conduit to an ambition, some thing or someone else.

And there, for the two kinds of desert, are two kinds of arrivals.

One is the showing up of a receptive person, you are the tenon and she the hole.

The other is less common and should be feared. There will always be a void in the center of the hole.

Safer to partner with the first. Jack and Gretchen were option Ones. Funny that the alphabet betrays the lack essential to The One.

O.

Option 1.

Safer that way.

Robert

September 2015, New York

I keep clothes at both my New York apartment and the house in France. I liked the ease of going to the airport with nothing but my laptop, wallet and a sleep aid, an upper and a pack of cigarettes.

I get a lot done on a transatlantic flight, finished my new book on the way here. Strangely, I'd been unable to work on another trip a few weeks ago. For some reason, I was caught up thinking about her. We had taken the Concorde together once, way back. I had gotten nothing done then either.

I used to write pages anticipating Olympia's notes in response. My favorite was, "Stop moralizing, you're over-correcting for the lack of integrity in your everyday being."

Five?

Ten years since she'd been gone.

Mathilde

September 2015, still New York

I often snuck out to the office library while the others went to lunch. I'd taken the job thinking that it would allow me to focus on route things, to pretend to be like them and easy.

Since I'd been a young girl, I'd always tried to dive into some kind of project to exorcise my anxiety. There was the fantasy of working in a research lab, keeping track of details with only one careful variable. Nothing I couldn't control. Charts. Tables. Graphs. Neat equations. Theories proven.

But, no.

My mother had always cautioned me against becoming any kind of artist. She didn't allow me to dance after the age of ten. It didn't matter that I was being recruited by a number of top ballet schools. I don't know why she'd taken me to class to begin with. My only clear memory of that time is that of her pulling back my hair one morning. Once she secured the elastic high on my head she'd turned the tail curling it into a snake-like coil, one bobby pin to secure the end. She pulled my hair and whimpered. I vaguely remember her saying something as she laughed at herself in the mirror. "I made you and I'll destroy you." Another mother would have offered comfort in place of self-congratulatory wit.

Something happened around that time that caused her to have to travel more often, always back and forth to France. My father would go too, at least for a little while. He said it was part of his diplomat work. I stayed with my mother's friend, Dorothy. She would come in from out of town to "watch" me. I never went anywhere. She drank a lot.

I was too young to drive so it became difficult for me to get to dance class. I thought it was unfair of my mother to not come up with a solution as she'd been a dancer until she gave it up. She'd never told me her version of the story, but my aunt said one day she just didn't show to rehearsal, and then she never went again. Unwavering decisiveness was one of her greatest talents.

Creative pursuits had to be relegated to after hours.

When I met Jack, I felt a shift in my own version of this mania. Even his physical presence calmed me. The all consuming "I'm-not-going-to-be-okay" subsided a little bit and in its place came a taste of the certainty that my mother had seemed to hold.

It was in September of last year that I cracked and began to write and collect research with intention, unsure of what form it would eventually take, images and anecdotes that lent evidence to my own crazy theories. I knew my critical writing needed work, that I matched up thoughts and words in a sophomoric way.

Like the game Memory.

To me, it made perfect sense: one side of the Memory cards are printed with a certain number, pairs of matching images—twin words, drawings, paintings, photographs—the other side something uniform.

This uniform side of the cards can be any color, any image, just all the exact same.

You place the cards face down in rows. You turn one over. Then, another. If they match, you put them aside and go again. If they don't, you turn them over and your playmate gets a try.

The strange thing about Memory, unlike cataloging proof in life, is that every round gets easier and easier.

Only recently, I'd begun saving images on my I-phone and photographs of relevant text. Sometimes they had been screen-shotted from the online original, and then again later on so that the time stamp of the digital file betrays its revisitation. I do this so that the picture appears in the camera "roll," easily accessible, at the bottom of the grid of stored images.

Unlike Memory, these images—the screen shots—do not match up objectively when laid on top of one another, rather they explain corollary phenomenon.

Gamer's choice. Pick your story.

In 1974, the performance and multimedia artist Carolee Schneemann made a book called "Cezanne, She Was a Great Painter." It contained ephemera of Schneemann's writing and notebooks from the '60s and '70s, including the script for her performance "Interior Scroll." The title comes from an anecdote she relates in which she decides that Cezanne is her mascot and must have been a woman, emphasis on "Anne." Here Schneemann makes her own verbal and visual pun. Cezanne himself played with the final syllable of his last name. "Ane" meaning donkey.

Donkey. Otay. Obsessed with stories. Don Quixote. Image and image maker. Schneemann used her naked body to attract the audience's gaze and then subvert it. In Fuses (1965) she records herself and her composer lover having sex.

Cezanne took a copy of Virgil when he went off to paint.

Someone once asked artist Francoise Gilot, one time Picasso muse and lover, her thoughts on Mallarme. She thought he was too obscure, not for everyone. Then, she told a story about him and Manet having eyes for the same woman, a demimondaine. That Manet consummated this desire, but Mallarme did not, preferring to imagine it. Perhaps he thought it would last longer that way.

"Impressionism," Gilot said and laughed.

In the introduction installment to Mallarme's compilation Divagations *"Autobiography," he writes about seeing Manet every day for ten years. He says, "…and people even speak of my influence, where in fact there were only coincidences. He brings up coincidence again saying that a writer has the excuse that any coherence found in the book is aided by its assembly, and perhaps, too, by always saying the same thing."*

It's true.

Also, true that talking about Mallarme may be cliche. And, talking about desire.

But, if part of desire is the urge to find a likeness in pursuit of making the self whole how do you pre-serve the lack to project imaginings? Unsustainable and irreconcilable.

The Uncanny seems to be a catch-all phrase for sensations accompanying evidence that there are others that are the same. This is why erotic desire often calls for novelty.

Longterm relationships lose the ability to reassure you that, by chance, the greater world will still show you this likeness.

The uncanny comes in many guises, all of which exist by virtue of not existing or having once been. For the uninitiated or rule-mad person, this results in the need to catalog and control, for systems and hierarchies.

* * *

Two weeks before traveling with Jack, I had gone to visit Tom in his studio. He'd invited me, which was an unusual move. We'd met one night at a dinner and I guess he had liked my vibe so he had said to email him and come by. I did. He usually gave people the address for a fake studio manager.

The tricky thing was determining whether one was meant to react feel seduced or repulsed by this arrogance of a young artist claiming to be important. Context was everything. Gretchen had fallen victim to the bad version of this on more than one occasion, mostly because she wanted to make something of her own and couldn't, and didn't realize her tenure as muse was for a limited time only. There were plenty of takers with a taste for pretty, moneyed girls who were looking for purpose and to piss off their parents.

I was a safe target and wise career ally. Tom was being courted by a number of galleries and equally as many transparent women.

The studio was minimal. He had one assistant who wasn't there when I arrived. Fair though, that many of his pieces were manufactured assembly line style by outside agents, far from this loft. There was paint all over the floor, but none anywhere near the single large canvas stuck with blue duct tape at its corners to the wall. The windows were blocked out with similar set ups. I had heard that he preferred to work through the night. There were a few stray pieces of clothing flung on a mustard couch nearby.

"Hey, com'ere," he called from the back room. I walked towards his voice as he came out wearing a baseball cap and an old flannel shirt. He also had on a pair of old jeans—real old jeans, not the expensive kind Will bought from that vintage dealer one of his model ex-girlfriends had introduced him to. He took my hand and led me to the backroom. Inside was a mess of books thrown on the floor among papers. There were two plastic lawn chairs set up in the back corner. I sat down.

"Tell me what's going on in here?" I asked pointing at one of the canvases.

"I honestly don't know," he said taking the seat next to me. I had the sense that he was holding back, testing me in some way.

My phone went off. I looked down. It was Jack.

"All okay?" he asked over text. It was late and I hadn't spoken to him after leaving the office. I covered the screen so Tom couldn't see.

He brushed my waist as he pulled my chair closer to his. There was an awkward but complicit silence.

"Smith passed."

Those were the only two words in the email we received.

Should we send condolences to Howard Smith's wife? To his dealer? It's strange he died, wasn't all that old. Fifty maybe?

Should we tell our clients to buy the work before news spreads? Tomorrow the Times would run his obituary.

Is it not cool to do a mass email?

We typed the subject: Smith Passed.

Maybe not.

At the very least, we should alert Mr. Wilson.

This espresso tastes disgusting, that last bit of sediment from the morning, lukewarm and thick.

We should email everyone. It's like that time Alice's mother forgot to tell her father the news she heard about an artist's late stage sickness. He was livid, saying he would have bought more works had he known.

She remembers him yelling, "Margaret, I can't stand you. You're too principled."

We didn't want to get in trouble. It would be easier and untraceable if we just went through all the names in our cell phones. We could send a mass text. We'll just call Mr. Wilson first.

Straight to voicemail. "Hi Guy, it's Us. Remember that Smith work we saw last week..." We weren't sure what to say. It would be tacky to mention his death in the message. We hung up and refreshed email.

Go away self doubt. What was that mantra we were supposed to repeat whenever we started to feel this way? Fuck. We hate talking to ourselves. It's cool no one else is in the office right now.

Alice's cell phone lit up with that rectangle of an incoming text. It was from Wilson:

"The Smith passed at auction this morning. Why are you always wasting people's time."

Robert

October 2015, outside Paris

It was a short connecting flight back from Switzerland. I thought a brief get away to the mountains would be good before Christopher arrived.

I had stayed in a small town where there were pointy roofs and blue night skies. An old friend ran the nearby foundation. We would walk to town in the evenings, to our favorite restaurant where we always ordered the fondue. The proprietress was an elderly lady who recognized me from years back. She asked where Olympia was.

"She's in Paris," I lied.

The woman had on a navy blue bandanna folded and wrapped around her head, tied below her ears. She was wearing a calico dress with a matching apron and white clogs. I don't think it was nascent dementia that made her scramble days. People always remembered Olympia.

Two years back, I'd gone to the Jura for a conference and the director had joked he'd invited me, hoping she'd come along. Looking back, the whole affair was rather obvious. An author does not often travel with his editor.

That night in Bern, we ate from an extra large iron pot of cheese as consolation. The familiar odor filled the restaurant and I'd tried to enjoy spearing the day-old bread, sticking it in dairy slop. After that dinner, I decided it was for certain time to return to France.

I had only my computer with me. No baggage claim, no run-ins with other people, just a straight shot to the cab once I got off the plane. It was only a few days until the residency began.

My house needed work before welcoming someone, especially someone who had competed for his place there. I had asked Mila, the house and groundskeeper, and the cleaner girl to get the guest room ready and move my desk into there. It was Mila who had discovered the rot in the antique table. I didn't have enough time to find something special and new, so told them to switch one desk for the other. It didn't occur to me to worry about the papers and effects, only where I would work. I remembered Olympia had liked to write out back in the garden.

Mathilde

October 2015, Munich

Jack was always good with me whenever I lost it, as if he had seen it coming. He often took me with him when he had work overseas, maybe to keep an eye on me. Made me think my father should have, could have, done the same. The last time, there had been meetings back in London and Warsaw, some sort of a policy deal and then a quick sojourn to Cannes. I'd been invited by a collector. Jack had been game, finding it all quite amusing. He would stay in the background, not vying for any kind of attention, observing all the while.

His skill in putting together deals and identifying opportunity came from quiet, knowing observation, discretion and diplomacy. When we first met, he'd explained to me that he was spending a lot of his time making the decision on which direction to go with his work. He had job offers from Deutsche Bank, Goldman Sachs, something with the UN and two other NGO's. I told him it didn't seem like a difficult choice. If he worked for the UN we could stay in New York and he could get experience and always move over to an NGO. It bothered me that he fixated on the other two, rationalizing a few years there, a few years here.

In the end, he saw the most value in not making a decision, rather going to London to help set up Cambridge's

Centre for Rising Powers at POLIS (Department of Politics and International Studies at Cambridge.) He argued that London would be like a little pod of protection for me. I applied to the Courtauld and was accepted, Gretchen said she'd come visit once a month. And we left. I had Jack and my studies, a safe house, library of distractions.

It was Jack who made the logical deductions, decisions and practical arrangements. He'd always done it for both of us, something I took for granted.

As usual, I was getting tired of sitting by myself working from a hotel parlor. The one in Munich was a strange place, only three floors and a green stone bar in the lobby. The same characters showed up every afternoon to order tall orange drinks and look out the rear window. I knew it was time to go when they started to greet me. One afternoon, as I sat in my usual spot, the tall red-haired policeman asked my name.

Jack had meeting after meeting and I didn't want to be left alone, because the writing had gotten out of control. Before we left New York, I'd taken out my mother's old notebooks, empty orange Clairefontaine's I'd found in the armoire.

Jack always seemed fine and I wanted a reaction. So, I decided to leave him. And anyway, I needed to get to Paris. Charles had called to tell me he wanted me there.

It was perfect that the auction house allowed me to move around, but it had its problems. I was there because

I wanted to try to do the same thing my mother had, remove myself from the creative game. She did it by decoding and recoding other people's work. I was herding objects.

Studying art history with the intention to go to work at an auction house had been an easy way to navigate my dueling impulses, still harboring a tiny void I hoped would go away. Because, when it widened, I felt a little less control. I wanted to try to be the perfect employee and foster relationships and have rules and follow them. And then, it turned out, there really aren't any.

Jack made a similar choice, and so for a while we had that in common. He liked protocols, things that slowed down his world. When I decided I had to leave him that day in Munich, I said it was for a true work assignment, and it was, one I would create when I landed.

There was talent and potential clients to visit. Work where relationships are the unspoken primary capital makes for a tricky skill set. I'd always thought best to be earnest, kind and clever. I'd been confronted with my own naivety. It felt like to be the desirable thing, you had to swan around without struggle. To be that woman, meant to allow its privileges to become entitlements.

Having the right eye, that elusive taste too often seemed to equate with accepting that wish fulfillment meant taking from someone else, and belonging meant another's exclusion. If I gave in and folded, I'd have no choice but to go back to writing, even if in an academic capacity. My fantasy of endless bureaucratic distractions would be blown up.

"I have to go to Paris," I announced to Jack as he was unfolding the International Herald Tribune that had been slipped under the door.

He nodded, picked up one of the two espressos he'd ordered, placing mine by my bedside for whenever I'd want it. "That's cool."

I was wearing one of his white button down shirts and a pair of his basketball shorts. They were so long they almost reached my ankles. He always packed extra. I never remembered my own casual clothes.

"Sure, whatever makes you happy." He didn't look away from the paper as he took another sip from the cup. Behind him was an arrangement of white roses from the hotel.

"Don't you want me to stay?"

"Whatever makes you happy."

"What makes *you* happy?"

"Mati, chill. Just be happy. I am fine with whatever you have to do." He wasn't ignoring me; he was managing me.

Jack was the only one who called me Mati. Everyone else called me Tilly, but more often Mathilde. They say it in two syllables: Meh Tilled, with an American accent. My mother had always loved this name. I miss her and all her stories.

I had wanted to ask her to explain them. But I knew not to. You didn't ask her for clarity. She was like a sphinx-oracle, said what she wanted and left you to sort it out. It was the same thing after the accident.

I know I will always be obsessed with Jonathan, or his absence. Like solving my mother's riddles, this would be something I'd never received confirmation on, no illumination, no answer. People always leave that way. In the wake, a corrosive wheel of thought asking what could have been done.

And then despite this hard-won lack of knowledge, we do the same thing to someone else.

I got up and went into the bathroom, knocking the side of the table spread with breakfast. Jack didn't look. Without closing the door, I threw his top onto the floor and then his shorts as well. I turned the faucet of the bathtub and the water came out in a loud burst, and still he didn't look.

"I'm going to leave tomorrow."

"That's cool. Do you need help?"

"I'm fine, but do you have any matches?"

"By those horrible flowers," he said. I left the water running and walked out naked. He smiled at me and folded the business section of the paper in half.

I found the matches and pretended to ignore his gaze.

I lit the candle and balanced it on the edge as I shut the water off. The bath was very hot and I waited for it to cool. I felt Jack watching me. Careful not to slide across the shiny white marble floor, I stood up and stepped onto the waiting mat. He had gone back to his reading.

I sank down into the water, placing my right hand out of sight. I touched skin and flicked my finger, stirring the pools of oil. They broke up, as the first knuckle on my hand showed from beneath the water again and again like driftwood frantic not to sink. I closed my eyes and pushed my finger lower where it was more wet than water.

October 2015, Paris

I didn't really have a plan when I landed at Charles de Gaulle. I had tried calling Christopher and his phone rang that overseas bleat.

I promised Sam to go the wig sellers in Paris and inquire about sourcing more hair. One of her old art school friends had told her about a shop down an alley way with lolling heads crammed into dirty vitrines. She'd said I should also check out the wigs, maybe bring home a nice auburn bob. "We could change things up a little."

Mathilde hadn't answered my question about Christopher. I knew she was angry that I would even consider him again. I texted her a second time.

"I get in tomorrow. Will be at the hotel by noon."

"See you then, unless I hear from Christopher."

"Wtf"

"He's in Paris. Forgot to tell you."

"..."

"Why is everything always so complicated? I just want to feel good and make stuff."

Mathilde

October 2015, Paris

When I decided I'd leave Jack and go to Paris, Gretchen decided to get on a plane and wait for me there. She had no obligations, no reason not to. She also knew through another friend that Christopher was there for some kind of residency. It was unclear how long it had been since they'd spoken. She still slept with Sam, liked being her studio wife, helping to make the wax limbs she used in her shows. On Tuesdays, Gretchen would spend hours applying real human hair which she sourced from assorted places to the glow-in-the-dark-pallor arms and legs.

"Can I ask you a question?" Gretchen texted me. This funny affectation always made me pause. It was so submissive or unnecessary. What it usually meant was, "Don't be annoyed with what I'm about to say."

"Go ahead. You know I hate when you do that."

"Have you heard anything about Christopher?"

Gretchen

October 2015, Still Paris

I had taken too many Klonopin and woke up in Mathilde's hotel bed in a massive cloud. Whenever I took the sleep aid, I always sent a message or an email that I didn't remember writing. Each pill had the effect of half a dozen tequila shots for me. It didn't really matter though, as I longed for that feeling when I could go under and not have to worry about tossing to fall asleep. It was a powerful thing to be able to regulate my own Circadian rhythms. I was proud of never being jet-lagged. Although, it felt like I was always low grade jet lagged. Sometimes, the pills left me with a narcoleptic head bob, especially if I woke up too soon. This had sabotaged almost as many friendships over dinner as I'd messed up via incoherent text. Whatever.

My current circumstances were hazy, not because of a chemical scramble. At least not from ingestible drugs.

Through online stalking, I'd found out that Christopher was in Paris working on his next novel at some new residency just outside of the city. He always said that I saw him through one book a few years back, but he also had a wife at that time. I'm not sure if she knew how to read, though.

He was the master of research. Everything was research. He wanted to do something, he called it research.

This included me, I think. The thing about fiction writers and research is that the lines become very sketchy. It can easily slip into a manipulation, as it often did with Christopher. He would reach out to an unwitting woman of sundry occupation demanding a coffee to "ask a few questions." He'd been doing research in Buenos Aires before coming to Paris.

I had always feared our written correspondence, not least of all because emails were everlasting. His tone was always hard to pin down. Was he playing me? Always half sincere, half mocking.

Back then, he always offered just enough that I couldn't cut him off forever. And when I thought I would be strong enough to ignore him, he always found a way back in. He never asked how I was doing or what my situation was, only if I remembered him or a simple, "Hi." Once I wrote back, he'd won. When he went silent for extended periods it corresponded with a new love interest or distraction. I knew this by now and still worried that one forgotten answer would be the last between us.

He made this strange dynamic impossible to end and created a reason I could never be all in with anyone else.

Mathilde saw it most clearly as she'd watched it from afar, for years. But, even she didn't know all the trouble he made.

Robert

May 2002, Berlin

When I met Olympia, she was wearing a navy blue tuxedo suit without a shirt underneath and a thick band of sapphires on the second finger of her left hand. I'd noticed her the moment she walked into the room.

I already knew who she was, but pretended otherwise. A well-respected American editor, the sort you hardly ever heard about any more, who cared about shepherding her writers through work and life, rather than her own self promotion.

Olympia was old school, but also avant-garde in this way that no one could really explain. Somehow she moved among the men in her tricky little world while simultaneously rejecting them. She was married with a daughter and still never missed a conference or deadline. Twelve hours after Mathilde was born, she had a manuscript and pen in hand. She slid around undetected until a book came out and then everyone talked about it, and indirectly her.

I was deep into a project that I knew Olympia was perfect for. It was a sort of farce, knowing and funny, but unusual in its non linear narrative. I followed her outside the party and pretended to fumble for a cigarette. It had been years since I'd had one. "You smoke?" I asked her.

"Yes, would you like…?" She took out a pack.

"Where did you grow up?" I asked.

She laughed. "Who are you?"

"Robert Northwell." I offered my hand. She laughed again.

"I know. I love your work. You should think about sending me your next book."

"Funny you should say that…"

We left together.

We had decided to stop at a cafe on the walk back to my hotel room. Olympia drank three Berliner Weisse, which impressed me. I made her laugh telling a story I'd just heard from a friend about two colleagues: an American academic named Charlotte and a French anthropologist called Serge.

When Serge first met Charlotte she was married to another academic who she had met just after she told her dissertation advisor that she had changed her mind about being with him. He had just left his wife.

Then, on a fact finding trip to Senegal, Charlotte met up with Serge, whom she'd known professionally for some time. Six months later she was pregnant with his child. And…

Olympia interrupted me, "God damn sociologists."

I decided then to make a play for her affection and professional guidance all at once.

"So what do you think?"

"I will need to read it first," she said and added. "You know I'm married, yes?"

"And you have a daughter?"

"That's right." She continued, "That means I won't fall in love with you. I mean, I could, but it won't mean anything. I won't leave my situation."

"Well, okay," I said. "Works for me."

"Can you imagine that meet cute?" Olympia had asked me as we lay in bed. "Two academics driven by—"

"You mean between the anthropologists?"

"Yes. The whole story reeks of Hollywood."

"But, it's true."

"Of course it is, because if it were made up the experts in social behavior wouldn't be neatly predictable."

"But, I had said they were anthropologists: this is very different. You make the mistake of calling them sociologists."

"Whatever. That's sort of faux-poetic and thin. There are good and bad guys only in the movies."

"Yes. Well, here we are."

I still have the paper Olympia slipped under my door after she read the project. She had left my hotel room very early that morning with a stack of papers under her coat. I knew she had to leave for the airport that afternoon. I was surprised to see the note when I came back early that evening.

I had no intention of joining my friend for dinner, but liked to commit to things and then, cancel last minute. And so, I had just missed her drop off. I remember turning around as if I expected her to be in the hallway. But she was gone.

I picked up the envelope and folded it in half. Despite my curiosity, I wanted to delay it all. I poured a glass of whisky from the coffer, and finished the peach liquid. After closing my eyes for a few minutes, I tore into the note. The words inside were written on a piece of scrap paper from the hotel's room service menu.

"Too self aware, too present. I want to forget you're the writer," she'd written.

Ironic and sincere.

PART II:
GOODS & SERVICES

Mathilde

October 2015, Paris

I didn't want to stay in the hotel room alone. So, I decided to wander outside until Gretchen arrived. It was past lunchtime and I still didn't have an appetite. I hadn't bothered to change my clothes from those I'd worn on the plane. The day was clear, but required a sweater and boots in case of rain.

The hotel was located on rue des Beaux arts, a left by the front door, a few paces and then, the looming gates of the art school. Students were still coming in and out for midday break. I bent my head and pushed through them. There was a toy shop down the street that had the small wooden animals my mother had given me as a child. The window filled with painted creatures the size of my hand: three extra large dinosaurs gnashing their teeth in the bottom vitrine, a row of hedgehogs crawling by. The sign on the glass said it was closed for lunch.

I went into the French pharmacy with its glowing green cross suspended over the door. I asked for the freckle fading cream an acquaintance wanted me to bring back. The pharmacist had never heard of it.

An old mannequin in another nearby window caught my attention. She had Anna Karina eyes, lined in black, pupils faded from the Paris sun. Her nose was tiny and pert like her breasts, though they were large relative to her waist and pin legs, a diamond with softened edges between her thighs. It was lit with the same dull gold that illuminated the shop beyond.

This girl wasn't like the other mannequins that lined the street, not like the distorted ones at the knock-off Spanish chain retailer dressed in cheap bar coats and tuxedo pants. This girl wasn't like the posed, perfect mannequins in the designer window, with black quilted spats and bags, bobbed pink hair—just for this season—and illustrated eyes. She also wasn't like the heads at the wig shop. Or the girls in the concept store down the way. They changed clothes a lot, sometimes wearing nothing but signature blue dots covering nipples and sex. This made me think of the girls back at the auction house office, colored blind spots.

This mannequin was wearing an expensive, handmade one-piece, blood red silk triangles at the top, outlined in *dentelle*, the French sort sewn by a woman in an atelier who too is thinking of a fantasy life. The straps were very thin and fell long in the back until just below the natural waist where the satin started up again. There were only strips of fabric holding at the back, so that a lover could look on in profile and see that demi lune that would fit in his hand. Three little satin covered buttons held slits on either side of the thighs. It was a unique piece, elegant and simple, more for the relationship between the onlooker and the object than the design. Consumed with staring back at her, I dropped my phone on the stone street. No one looked, not even the shop woman inside pretending not to see. I picked it up and wiped the screen, one big fissure through the stock wallpaper.

This lingerie shop was one of those old one-off Parisian stores you had to buzz to be let in. I stopped to check if anyone was watching me. Then, touched the gold button and the lock let go. I went inside.

"Puis-je vous aider?" The woman asked without looking up. She was trying to tack buttons through silk rouleau loops on a nightdress. Her hair was blond and messy with volume at the crown. She had a thick black ribbon tied around her head. Her part was deep over her left eye, the eye that almost looked up when I walked in. There was a big gap between her two front teeth that could be seen when she smiled, which she did when I couldn't answer her. I was embarrassed to be there, like I was doing something wrong.

How funny that I'd passed this way years before on one of our rare mother-daughter trips, that I'd stopped to stare and my mother had hurried me along. We'd been to visit some church just before and were en route to a cafe for the hot chocolate I'd been promised.

Later that night, I noticed lavender bags in my mother's suitcase, embroidered with the name of the store.

After watching me with disdain, the woman picked a pack of cigarettes from under the set of drawers in front of her and went to the door. "Excusez-moi," she said and left me inside.

I felt a kind of relief to be there alone, among all the lace and silk things. There was a wooden rack to my right filled with multiplying and shrinking blue and whites: a slip dress, a robe, a camisole, a bra. There was a settee with cream pillows in between the alcoves and a muslin bust at the base of the stairs to the backroom. Next to her, a mannequin wearing a top made of two lace triangles, a sheer mesh diamond at its center.

At the back of the shop, there was a display of black silk covered suspender style garters. It was the kind of belt that I remembered reading about in a book of short stories my mother kept hidden, a nondescript cover tucked in the back of her bookcase. The first story I'd opened to was one about a young girl and an older woman who makes her wear one and nothing else. In my favorite scene, the girl is told to finger a flower and then carry the stem in her garter belt beneath a white dress.

The woman came back into the shop and shut the door lightly behind her. She saw me holding the belt and raised a gold banded finger with its red painted nail. I handed it to her and nodded. She brought it behind a table and pulled out a lavender bag.

Everyone said I should be happy. Jack was handsome, perfect and loved me completely. I wasn't thinking of him as I made the selection.

Calm, studied, diplomatic Jack.

A car alarm went off outside. And still, he wasn't the one in my mind.

In 2004, at the Tate Liverpool, Mike Kelley restaged *"The Uncanny"* show he'd originally put together for *Sonsbeek 93*. In the new catalogue introduction, Kelley writes that he is acutely aware that the landscape of contemporary art has changed in the nine years since the first show.

The ubiquity of polychrome figurative sculptures is one example, nearly a decade ago they were much rarer and therefore even less familiar. Consequently, in another part of Kelley's introduction, he explains that his *"harems"*—collections of objects he's amassed to represent the impulse to collect—must always be shown in context for fear of them losing meaning. They are less about the objects on their own, aisles and rows in vitrines.

He says this can be done simply by providing footage of a walk through of the whole exhibition. It doesn't matter so much what the contents of the cases are, rows of squeaky dog toys, instruments to a member of a noise band as Kelley once was, spoons, or business cards.

The objects are not important.

In context, they are the urge to pin down a messy world. An accompanying video mandated with future displays of *"harems"* assures Kelley control over interpretation of his work, not dissimilar to the kingdom one seeks when amassing things in the first place.

Unsurprisingly, Kelley had a false career-start as an aspiring novelist. He soon turned to making art: objects as sculpture. These collections, "harems," could be read as resurrecting familiar sensations and repressed desires.

Robert Gober's Untitled Leg, (1989): out of the wall comes a wax limb severed below the knee, its black polyester pant leg cuffed to reveal human hair on the leg. The skin has a honey-colored dead pallor. It wears a gray cotton sock and a scuffed brown dress shoe. There are tiny hairs all over it.

Object instead of word communicates known strangeness. In The Art of Cruelty, *Maggie Nelson writes, "Psychoanalysis gets interesting when it shifts the focus from making us more intelligible to ourselves to helping us become more curious about how strange we really are. And so, I would argue, does art."*

Perhaps the critics—readers—even, lend more complex, more desirable interpretations or intention, its own ecstatic act. It was from the onlooker that Kelley came to learn about his own work. "That's what led to my interest in repressed memory syndrome and the fear of child abuse. This wasn't my idea—I was informed by my viewers that this is what my works were about. I learn a lot from what my audience tells me about what I do."

* * *

Gretchen had told me she would be at the hotel bar sitting on one of the green banquettes beneath the Cocteau drawings. We'd been there before together, years ago. I had saved all my money from working at the cafe on campus to take a trip to Paris. She had insisted she join and that we stay where her family always stayed. It took her a while to convince me to let her pay for it. I eventually agreed, newly single, happy to not be alone. Most mornings I woke up early and let her sleep and she'd come downstairs and find me on the sofa.

Years later, I requested the hotel on work trips. I found Gretchen in our spot staring at her phone.

I placed my bags on the leopard-carpeted floor next to the destroyed Belgian loafers she'd taken off. "Why did you take your shoes off? Do you want to put your stuff upstairs?"

"Can I order a drink first?"

"Why not call down?"

"But I want one now. What'd you buy?" Gretchen pointed to the purple bag.

"Come on." I picked up her backpack and pulled her off the couch. Gretchen was wearing a gray hooded sweatshirt and tight jeans. She bent over to slide on her battered loafers, crushing the backs with her heels. "You only have a backpack?"

"What else would I need?"

"I don't know, maybe a change of clothes?"

"I had some stuff sent ahead of time."

"What a farce. You need a new pair of shoes."

"I'm the kind of girl who travels light." She passed me on the stairs as she started taking two at a time, bounding until her slip on fell off. There was a small bang as it hit the marble floor.

"Shit."

"What?"

"I just dropped my Belgian three flights down."

"You're insane."

"You go ahead, I'll get it." I climbed the rest of the stairs to our room. She stopped at the front desk to flirt with the bellboy, asking him to find the three boxes she had sent before her.

On the hotel website they called 44 the "Violette Le Duc room." It was a dark box with red flecked wall paper and matching velvet curtains. French doors were the only source of daylight when this heavy fabric was secured with oxblood bows. Over the bed, there was an enormous oval mirror trimmed in gold-painted wooden molding. To the left, one of those antique desks with tiny drawers that hid poison. I dropped Gretchen's backpack by the door and took my own things straight to the bathroom. Unlike the bedroom, there was less of a show. The tiles were painted matte yellow and green, naked cream ones in the shower, a big porcelain tub with a blackened silver faucet. I bent down to turn the water on. It rushed out splashing my face and clothes.

More bourgeois decor

On the way out of New York City, there's a motel with a tiny light-up Eiffel tower on top. It's called the Paris Suites, its rip-off monument seen from the expressway, neon flash at night.

The concrete building has a thick windowless tower with the white letters *H O T E L* propped like sculptures on the roof. There's an archway of white bricks leading to the marble lobby where the walls are painted with thin veins. The ticket counter where you pay for your getaway is a slab between an aquarium cut in half like the woman in a magician's show. On either side of the window, there are pillars in different classical style than the rest of the house references. They line the demi-trapezoids filled with googley-eye goldfish and glowing purple light.

Not far, two plastic mastodon tusks stand on the night porter's desk. Two wavy geodes are below, on the floor on either side, like dancing drunk cross sections their skin hard and white, their guts jagged and purple. Each of these is bordered by a gold crusted commode.

Across the way, in front of the mirrored wall is a similar set up in reverse order, from left to right: an amethyst crystal, a gilded pedestal, a squat centerpiece with painted-on marquetry and a bronze-colored sculpture of a lion. There's a mermaid in a window *vitrine, a silver crocodile fastened to a flat wall, and a herd of winged chimeric statues.*

The lobby of the carefully decorated Paris Suites is filled with objects made by trompe l'oeil wizardry: slices of precious materials glued on to matte under layers.

In each bathroom, there is a red jacuzzi with two control panels. One says "massage" in clear script. You can see the cameraman's reflection as he tapes the glass enclosed pod. He holds a camcorder. The bath has a round, cherry lacquer base and sliding doors with frosted bamboo designs. The top of the spa pod looks Sci-Fi with twinkling lights. For a moment, in the video, there is a stop in the stark bathroom, an unbroken stretch of white sanitary tape holding the toilet seat down. By the foot of the bed, slippers embroidered with tiny Eiffel Towers are wrapped in plastic too. In this online clip, the cameraman is never fully revealed, only glimpses of him in reflective surfaces.

Inside a Paris Suite, you can find an ode to an English Romanticist painter and East Asian symbols of virtue. Outside, a copy of an iron structure put up once for World Fair, meant to be a transient thing, taken down in twenty years. It now attracts more visitors than almost any other global tourist attractions, is reimagined in tiny souvenir keychains, and somehow has become symbolic for some kind of escapist romance.

The personal rewriting of a critical moment in anyone's development becomes personal mythology. When a doubt or obstacle arises, manipulated facts allow for suspended disbelief, solution or comfort to longing or desire or impotence.

On the Paris Suites website, the Queens destination is also known as the "Little Ritz Hotel," very close to the "famous US Open" tennis courts. Here, there is also a virtual tour that allows you to peek into one of the double suites. Orchestral muzak plays in the three minute clip, which begins in the bedroom. The videographer scans from the bed frame with blue-brushed velour blanket tucked in tight to two lamps with bases of red glass on the side table. A pan across a beige curtain shows the lamps again, reflected in the big screen television, two glowing, fuzzy shapes on blank black tableau. There is a painted landscape above the bed done in thick oils and framed in shiny gold plaster. The site shows a picture of this picture and its little blurry sunset leaking into the rest of the frame within a frame.

We were at our desks, all in a row. Red, blue, yellow and blue again. There was one empty seat. It was nearing the end of the day. How lucky to sit and wait and surf the Internet when frightening things were happening in the great big world.

"She's here now."

"How do you know?"

"I heard Charles tell someone on the phone that she would be available for a meeting."

"I can't figure any of it out."

"What's there to figure out?"

"What makes her so special? I don't think she's from a fancy family. But still Charles watches her, takes great interest in her."

"He thinks she can get him the work. Something from Tom Belier, I think. There's a very long waiting list and even if you make it, there's little logic to being the chosen one."

"Who are you explaining this to? We all understand the system."

"Is he single?"

"Do you think she sleeps with him?"

"I heard she slept with Will."

"I don't know she's not really his type."

"His type? He has no type. There was Lakshmi, then Gretchen, then Brigid, and Tara."

"You're forgetting the cohesive strand."

"Every one of those girls is from a wealthy family; every one of them playing that faux Bohemian vibe."

"But, what about Gretchen? She seems so—so—I don't know, 'dirty?'"

"Dig a little deeper."

"Isn't she really close with Mathilde?"

"She is."

"How does she fit in with the other girls?"

"She's the penultimate Will conquest. Fake working class roots, chill vibe and obscene money in the bank."

"Why'd he leave her?"

"She left him. She's not as dumb as she pretends to be. Apparently some writer guy."

"Will tells people he flew her to meet him in Marrakesh just to break up with her. Says he wanted a romantic breakup."

Silence.

"Do you think Mathilde's fucking Charles?"

"He would never."

"Didn't we just go over this?"

"You know we talk about the same things over and over again, all the time."

Mathilde

October 2015, Paris

I lay on the bed, naked, looking at Gretchen eyes closed, flat out. She had come back to the room, ordered a bottle of champagne and fallen quiet. I was relieved as I wasn't sure I could hear anymore about Christopher.

It was only just past five o'clock, if I didn't go outside again soon, I was at risk of giving in to jet lag. The room was small and it would have been difficult to get dressed without waking her, except she was notoriously hard to wake up.

There was a t shirt and a long black skirt on the top of my suitcase. I pulled them on and went back into the bathroom to look in the little mirror. My hair was messy and half wet. I pushed it behind my ears and quickly did some uneven eyeliner. Two more minutes and I was down the spiral stairs, out the door and into the street, leaving Gretchen to sleep.

I decided to go have a drink at the nearby cafe. It was close enough to walk, though the sky was darkening. So, I slipped into a taxi.

The cafe was just past the looming Benedictine Abbey at Place Saint-Germain Des Prés. I had been by the church a few times, yet never gone in. I'd been on this path before not only with Gretchen, but with my mother years earlier.

There was a bookshop around the corner from the church and across the street from the cafe. All not that far from the arcade with the toy and lingerie shops. It was all very familiar but new because of the small changes that had happened over the years. And the larger ones. This added up visually to a dusting of elemental damage or shuffling of real estate. I was unsettled not because of evidence on the streets, but my own internal shifts, the changed spectator.

My mother had always avoided the book shop. She said she didn't want to think about work while she was with me. It always fascinated me why she refused to go in. I have trouble remembering most details of our trips to Paris. They seem so long ago. It's a selective memory thing. Details will come forward when they match up with the present. There had been nights when she would leave me asleep in the hotel and go out somewhere but always be back when I woke up. I'm not sure why I never asked for an explanation.

I decided to go into the book shop instead of the cafe. There were tables spread with books with neutral covers, blue typeface repeating in patterns across a grid of cream rectangles. There were some shelves along the walls, filled with shiny paperbacks. The art books were to the right and there was a small erotic section in a cabinet in the center. Most of the other books were arranged by theme or author in tidy stacks. I picked up one of the novels on the center display. I'd seen these editions often as a child scattered all over my house, so different than books in school or at the library. A salesperson looked me up and down before asking if I needed help. I shook my head and continued browsing, stopped to pick up an issue of some arts magazine.

"Mathilde?" a familiar voice said my name. I got nervous and hid it behind my back and turned around.

Tom was standing in front of me.

"What are you doing here?" I asked him. My tone came out harsher than I wanted it to.

He laughed. "I didn't mean to startle you."

"No-no, I mean, it's nice to see you, but I didn't realize you were here."

"I needed a book." I laughed and started to explain. He stopped me, "I'm here to install a show."

There was an awkward silence. We hadn't spoken since that day in the studio. I wanted to ask him why he hadn't mentioned the show but realized I hadn't mentioned my own travel, that this trip had been a last minute call from Charles. "Do you want to go next door and have a drink?" he asked.

"Sure," I said and put down the magazine. He took my hand which surprised me and we walked out. I let go as soon as we exited onto the street. Night was beginning to fall, but I could see all the passerbys clearly, their clothes, their shopping bags, and their stares.

"What's up?" he said as if nothing had happened. I didn't know what to say.

"W-would you want to come with me for a moment?" I asked without explanation.

"Where?" Tom laughed again looking confused.

"In there." I pointed to the abbey across the way.

He didn't seem to think it was an odd request. And had he, I wouldn't have known what to tell him; I would have seemed too familiar. I thought it was a good short term diversion. He didn't take my hand again as we walked towards the entry way together.

It was a wide stone vaulted transom that separated the back of the church from this entrance's antechamber. I looked at Tom as he led the way. He was dressed in the same outfit he'd been wearing at his studio. His hair was matted at the back and fly away on top and he looked more tired than usual. I walked behind him careful to lift my skirt instead of letting it drag on the cold stone floor. He turned around to make sure I was following him. Every one of each of our movements felt studied and self aware, the way they do between people who don't under-stand their standing with one another. The haunting music piped across the stale air added to the dis ease of the scene.

Part of me wanted to explain to him that my mother had once taken me to visit many of these eerie churches along the old pilgrimage route from Chartres. And how I'd had grown to associate the Benedictine chants playing from CDs with a kind of instant sadness and chilly intro-spection.

My mother had been an atheist, albeit one obsessed with religious paraphernalia and oddities. On that one trip to Paris she'd taken me to see one of the incorruptibles, a saintly body seemingly preserved—embalmed—by the psychic quality of its departed.

"It's just because they were good?" I had asked my mother as she stared at the dead body under glass. I pressed her. "Is it because that lady was good that she won't die?"

"She's dead." And that was all Olympia said by way of explanation.

There is a picture of our Anne—Schneemann—performing "Interior Scroll" in Mike Kelley's artist's book Vaseline Muses. The original photograph was of her standing on a table painted with mud, pulling paper from her vagina. In some stills, she is reading from the script. This one is blurry, the scroll looking like an umbilical cord at first glance.

The book's alternative title is "Why I Got Into Art." Kelley talks about how it was naked women that first attracted him to the art world. Every picture is re-photographed using a camera lens covered in petroleum jelly, vaseline. Kelley talks about "the moment of genesis of our sexual fiction," of having the historic luck to come of age when a very particular female masterminds the media.

John Baldessari's Prima Facie (Third State): From Aloof to Vapid, 2005 features a film still of the profile of a pretty woman in faint peach sepia tones. This is spliced with a white rectangle box and two columns of text in alphabetical order. The first starts with "aloof," and the last ends with "vapid." In between are "dispassionate" and "stony."

The writer Eve Babitz once called out "the Hollywood everything in which the more vulnerability and ineptness you project onto the screen, the more fame, money, and love they load you with." To her argument, you don't so much as need to believe in the character but that the person on screen is not *themselves, but a vessel. Success is found when the projection of the audience can fit comfortably in the body of work or the pretty little body of the avatar.*

Emile Zola, friend and confidante of Cezanne, once wrote about sexual attraction in reference to mannequins. Before industrial production of such things, necrophilia the unspoken stand in.

Body, sculpture, body, sculpture.

In 1903, Rainer Maria Rilke, who notably assisted the sculptor Auguste Rodin, wrote in an essay that sculpture had become "homeless." Humans were "wandering people," no longer keeping house, museum or collection in one location.

Imagine Babitz, all pneumatic beauty and sharp wit, comes back with sing song words, "The ones that get furthest carry a lighter load." The pin up screen star and blank-eyed Roman antiquity offer ingress, as does the hot performance artist-sinner or dead saint. The seduction is not in the narrative, but the lack of one.

Robert

October 2015, outside Paris

"He is finally here," Mila yelled to me. I had been expecting Christopher a few hours earlier.

Starting the residency, meant bringing other writers to me, when all I wanted was for everyone to go away. Christopher had already annoyed me. I wanted him to feel the error in his lateness. Because of the delay, I was in my running uniform, an old T shirt and sweatpants, the kind with a white drawstring and gathered ankles. I had wanted to exercise before his arrival. (I'm old. But I run the park every day, sometimes a 5K.)

I stopped on the landing to watch him through the window. He was tall, nearly the same height as myself. His hair was thick and black with premature white highlights. He wore it long enough that it curled, falling over his ears. Something was holding him back from coming straight to the door. He looked behind, as if being followed. The sky had turned a dirty clamshell color and the clouds broke only a pinhole of light. He moved to stand in the shadow on the stoop so that his green oil skin hunting jacket looked black and the white collar of his shirt neon.

"Welcome," I said as I opened the door. "I'm Robert."

"Hello, Robert," Christopher replied, dropping his bag to offer his left hand.

"Do come in." He paused and fiddled with his phone before going inside. Mila swooped in and grabbed his luggage.

"Uh, thank you for having me. Is an honor to be with you."

"I look forward to hearing more about your work. Please follow me." I led the way to the back of the house. "I'd like you to meet Mila. She's a lovely friend who works here."

"Enchante," Mila said from behind us, weighed down.

"Hi," he said without turning around.

"The kitchen is yours at any time. Help yourself to whatever. There will be meals made three times a day. Feel free to eat in your study, but I do recommend taking a small break. Do you run, by chance?" I asked.

"Not really," he said, adding, "what's your policy on guests?"

"What do you mean?"

"I'd like to have a friend, you know a lady friend, come by."

"By all means," I caught myself before admitting my dismay. "I won't be here very often and your time is your own. In fact, I'm about to head out."

"Is it possible to have a coffee?" Christopher looked back at Mila. I was growing more annoyed.

"With pleasure." She gave me a look and dropped the bag in the entryway.

"You will like this room," I said. "There are windows all out onto the back of the yard and thick curtains that can be drawn if you prefer very little light during the day. My room is upstairs. Please take my number should you need anything. You know we have no internet service and I would like you to please try to keep your phone in airplane mode. But, of course, do as you like. If you want to receive post, the address is, as you know, eleven rue d'Alsace 78100."

"Thank you." Christopher offered his hand. I ducked out closing the door behind me.

It felt strange to know that someone was finally staying in the guest room. When I'd bought this house fifteen years ago, I'd made sure there was an extra bed. I'd hoped to share the place with Olympia, that she'd leave things here.

Even her daughter Mathilde would come by.

I planned on asking her in a letter, as a kind of written proposal having kept the house a secret from her, knowing she probably wouldn't approve of it.

"No one really needs more than one house," she'd say.

We only had Paris. I rarely saw her when I was in New York, which was fine as I was busy. It did stoke my curiosity that she wouldn't even try. Our routine was her to offer lunch and me to decline and tell her I'd send pages when they were ready. Some strange performance.

Now, all I had was this arrogant young man to keep me company. The residency had come about in part as a memorial to her, though no one knew. It was a way for me to make use of the impractical space, to offer something back.

G-d, I miss her.

There would be so many times I would see something or hear something that I'd want to tell her. She'd understand why it mattered. Not that it was funny or smart or surprising, just that it was a shared reference.

This would have been easier to do via cell phone or email or all the things that had come around since our romance. When she was alive, I kept a log of references and malapropisms to tell her whenever I saw her. I still keep it.

We had a word game that we'd play in bed sometimes. She would lie with her left hand on my stomach, right hand behind her head as we tried to make one another laugh.

None of that changed that Olympia already shared her life with someone. I wondered if that man would understand the way I did all the incommunicable things about her.

A year into our affair, I realized something that should have been obvious. Having all seven shared days and nights would eventually lose its novelty. All those fine, mysterious moments I imagined would be pencilled in.

I was so in love with her, suddenly aware that who I was in love with wasn't her at all.

Mathilde

October 2015, still Paris

I walked faster and Tom followed me. I could feel his gaze going along my back. A small sign hung over the metal bin next to us. It had once said "Offrandes pour les Cierges," but letters had been scratched out and added.

Offerings for Candles to Offerings for Virgins. "Offrands pour les Vierges."

Candles for a donation to light in memory of someone who has passed.

I took five Euros out of my purse and dropped them in the padlocked box. Tom watched as I picked a taper and stopped for a moment feeling his hand at my shoulder. He reached into his pocket and offered me his lighter. I urged him to do it by flicking my chin and then, placed the thin candle in the glow and the wick caught fire. Tom brought the light to the bottom and it took me a moment to realize why he was doing this, melting the base so it wouldn't tumble from the candelabra. I stuck it in an empty bronze cup and it hardened there. Wax tenon in brass hole. I looked at him. He couldn't hear me thanking him or the secular prayer I offered for my mother.

"Where to now?" he whispered in my ear.

"Do you want to go back to your hotel?" He nodded and we walked through the church in single file.

As soon as we were outside, he was quick to be clear he wasn't presuming anything. "I think you will like to see the place. It's where Twombly used to stay and some other painters and jazz musicians."

"What's it called?"

"La Louisiane."

"You know Carolee Schneemann recorded the sounds in 'Meat Joy' by dangling a microphone out of one of its windows, down to the market stalls below."

I didn't tell him that my hotel was just around the corner.

We walked in silence. Our arms occasionally brushed one another. I had to mind my skirt. There were puddles everywhere from the rain.

The facade of La Louisiane was unassuming, locked between two other buildings, a pharmacie and an open air fruit seller, directly across from the butcher's stall. In front, were parked a number of scooters. I remembered that someone had told me that the digits on the license plate corresponded to where the driver was from.

All five ended in three eights. Three times eight = Twenty four.

Inside Tom's hostel, there was no doorman, just a disgruntled boy sitting behind a desk and an outdated pinned to the wall, rough stone foundation pillars in the sitting room, two old desktop computers for Internet access and standard supply issue floor covering. "It's not very fancy," Tom said. "Probably not up to your standards." His delivery a dig to me, not him.

Still, I followed up the stairs. They were carpeted in a worn pattern of diamonds and brown flowers falling inches short of the wooden steps at either side, tacked in place by gold rods. We went into his room and sat together at the edge of the bed.

Neither of us closed the door.

"Did you see the butcher's shop out front?" Tom asked looking at the floor, his hands all over searching for cigarettes.

"Yes?"

"I'm a little obsessed with it, with the idea of them, classic old school butcher shops."

"You mean like Francis Bacon?"

He laughed, "Sure—but not really. Although, I love that story of why he used the syringe in the painting to pin the man to the chair?"

"I read that in that book of interviews. The Sylvester one."

"I know this older man, a pretty well known artist, who has admitted to me that he stays quiet not because he isn't, as assumed by the public, a humble, work-obsessed talent who shies away from attention, but because he waits to hear the theories and criticisms, figuring out his intention ex post facto."

"That's not all of it. He understands the power differential in refusal, or whatever."

"I guess. The work isn't fully formed until he's picked out what to co-opt. And somehow, partly by luck and partly by calculated intent, he's managed to have everyone buy his myths."

"This is less interesting to me, unless it's because he veers towards idealism. Ambition is the dark side. Everything else, everyone else, every critic, every dealer, every friend-enemy, will have a proprietary narrative. Gretchen used to date this horrible writer guy who wrote all these essays about the male artist, his own abstention from self promotion and what it meant to be an honorable man…"

"I thought she dated girls? This was an old boyfriend?"

"I mean that's relative." I said. "The 'that he was an old boyfriend' part," I specified. "Can we order some wine?"

"There's no room service here," he said and smiled. "I'll run out and grab some. Sit tight?"

I nodded. It wouldn't have been wise to begin to be so personal with him. I remember Jack telling me to be careful about sharing too much of my life with those in my work world.

Buy and sell. Manufacture connection.

But I had nothing else to offer.

We'd gone to lunch, coffee, around the corner as Charles had left early for the day. Our usual tiny red square table was taken, so we sat at a green rectangular one. Two of us in chairs and the other two in the facing pink velvet booth. Four half filled cups sat on matching saucers in front of us, cooling off. No one looked up as we reached for them. Eight arms, a phone appendage on every second one.

"Charles says he wants three A+ works by Tom."

"He will take whatever he can get though."

"There's only a few days before we go to London."

"So much can happen in a day."

"Yes, but not the impossible."

"There has never been one at auction. Maybe just once in New York, but other than that."

"No one is giving those up."

"Why does he care? We have a full roster of everything else."

"He's a hunter. It's that mentality. Didn't you read that piece in the Times?"

"Which one?"

"The one about men and the hunt."

"That Neanderthal discovery?"

"It was an op-ed: The Art of the Hunt."

"Good title, like a painting."

We all paused and thought about this for a minute. Then, collectively started buzzing again.

"Mathilde may pull through."

"Good luck to her."

"Are you going to eat that?" The waiter had brought a red foil-wrapped chocolate square.

"No."

"Can I have it?"

"Go ahead."

"I'll break it. Watch." We stared as Alice slammed the metallic bit against the table. When she tore it open, the bar was divided into five pieces, four nearly identical in size.

"How did you do that?" She shrugged.

We each reached for a piece, leaving the tiniest one alone.

Mathilde

October 2015, Paris

When Tom came back to the room he was carrying two mismatched plastic cups he got from the kid sitting at the concierge and an opened bottle of red wine.

"I hope this is okay?" he said.

I accepted the cup with the crack on its side. "It's great."

"I used to drink bottles of this when I worked here all last year." He paused and lit another cigarette. His twin bed had a fitted sheet tucked in tightly at the corner, its duvet rolled up like some kind of flat pastry. "First off, why are you here?"

"Charles wanted me to come. He said he needed me to be here to meet with some potential clients and consignors before the preview. And to try and get a few more works."

"Some girl from your office called the studio."

"I didn't know you had a studio number," I said.

"Well, my cell. She left a message asking to meet with me."

"Oh, what did you say?"

"I haven't returned the call."

I nodded. He got up to open the window. It had a metal latch which he had to lift to release and then push open the two large panes. Back lit by the street lamps, he stood there paused as if waiting for me to ask him for something. Someone walked by the open door and then, two more men. I kicked it closed.

"Where is your husband?"

"He's in Munich for work."

"What does he do?"

"I don't want to…"

"Fair enough."

"What about your parents?" It was a funny leap in conversation.

"What about them?"

"What's the story?"

"My mother died in a car accident over a decade ago now. My father passed away a few years back."

"Oh, shit. I'm sorry." He sat down and pushed aside the caterpillar loop of bedding.

"It's fine. And yours?"

"My mother's a nurse and my father is a professor at the local university."

"Where?"

"Chicago."

"Right. University of Chicago?"

"Yeah." He put down his cup. And tried to put his arm around my back.

"I should get going," I said expecting to feel relief, instead I wanted to take it back after I'd said it. He pulled open the door. I downed the last of the wine in the plastic cup.

"No, I'll stay," I said, pulling up the hem of my black skirt so that I could sit back on the bed on my knees.

"Are you sure?" he asked.

"Yes," I said, a slight dizziness and rush. "Do you have a bath in here?" I heard myself ask.

Tom gestured to the hall. "It's communal."

He followed me into the dark hallway. I turned around and put both arms in the air questioning in either direction.

"Left," he said, close behind me. I pushed the scratch-graffitied door open and we both went inside. He pulled the string hanging from the ceiling, lighting up the room. There was a bath, a shower and three stalls, all dirty cream. And a strange lounger with woven strands of dark and pale blue plastic.

"Can I run it?" I asked looking at the cracked tub. He seemed concerned at first and then smiled a little, locked the main door and sat down on the beach chair.

"Whatever you want." I undid the metal wand from its cradle and let it fall on its rusty centipede coil into the waiting base. The hot water came out, the mouth sputtered and then flowed fast and easy. Neither of us said anything. I undid the tab on my skirt and pulled it off. He helped me with my shirt. Then, stopped short. "Are you sure?"

"I don't know," I heard myself again. He sat down again and stared at me. I had on a pair of underwear, satin bows tying at each hip. I took his hand and pulled him up again behind me.

I bent down to test the water, pushing my upper thighs into him. He placed his hands around my waist, grew hard and pressed himself into me, slipping his fingers under the ties and pulling them loose. I allowed this, but did not turn, instead stepped forward into the bath. He stepped back again and watched.

I sank down into the water so that only my nipples showed just above the meniscus of the tub. He undid his pants and stepped out of them. Without unbuttoning his shirt, he pulled it overhead. I then looked over at him. He was swollen and intent, climbing into the bath, pushing me to sit up so he could sit behind.

There was not much room in the old porcelain thing, he slid into me. I inhaled sharply and lifted my left leg to turn around and face him, without losing him. And then I rose in and out of the water. He helped me, his hands at my hips, raising me up, then down, then up again without taking his eyes from me. My eyes were closed.

And before long, he'd finished inside me, washed me with those same hands, then got up out of the water and wrapped himself in a towel. "Here," he said, tying his around his waist and offering me a new one open in the air. I stepped out and he closed it around my shoulders. He bent over to kiss my waist, then, lifted me over his shoulder to go to the bedroom. Balancing me, he used his free hand to unlock the door. No one was around. I was sure he could feel my stomach beating under his hand. The same hand pushed against the lower small of my back when I was face down on the bed, he on top of me. We were quick then, still.

It was so intimate because I didn't know this person at all.

* * *

In a note found written by artist Donald Judd, he says: "I could make an evaluative scheme, which is important, but borders on taxonomy, and again doesn't say everything." He argues that humans crave knowledge that their world is knowable. "It's not good to ignore this desire, since it's behind logic and science, but it can be understood that it will never be fulfilled and perhaps should not be."

He continues, "Anyway, the unfulfillment of desire is the human condition."

This somehow is similar to John Berger describing artist Cy Twombly as the "master of verbal silence."

Some of his works feature scrawled all caps letters of Greek and Italian mythological names. Venus 1975, "Venus" in red letters with a swirling flower, the background a list in graphite that begins, "Aphrodite."

Apollo 1975: "Apollo" in blue, two lists below. The one on the right features English words for animals, "Grasshopper," the last. But, these are words on a painted picture. They are not offered to explain.

These nods to antiquity conjure goddesses or cross associations within the viewer based on a certain set of references that took hold early in his or her life, or past lives, or learned through privilege. Even if they mean nothing that can be spoken, the shapes of the letters and the lists create a game.

Twombly also makes use of misspellings throughout his work to play with the viewer and her assumed mastery of the work. There is a story of the wonders of interpretation and the lack of accuracy in letters, of the perils of misguided translation featuring Freud.

He once mistranslated the Italian name of a bird in an old text to the German word for vulture. There are various theories on who did this and which text Freud carried over the mistake from, but no matter. It is what launched Freud to explore the role of the vulture in certain mythologies, and subsequently create lasting arguments. This is important because of its own doubling, explaining the fallible nature of letters. It is perfect that such a mistake would go on to inform the course of psychoanalysis and the exploration of desire.

Everything written here is the same, subject to a slight change and there is no longer the superimpositions that provide its scaffolding.

Is there a proprietary narrative? The story went something like that. Maybe I remember it wrong.

* * *

October 2015, still Paris

We lay there together for what felt like a long time. I was half drunk and in and out of a light sleep. When I woke up, the room was dark, but Tom was staring straight at me.

"Hi."

"Hi," he said and grinned.

Then silence as he looked past me deciding what to say. "I probably should head to work." It had been a long time since I'd had this kind of exchange. I'd forgotten how it felt to be left in someone else's bed.

"What time is it?"

"Like eleven p.m."

"I'll walk out with you."

"No, stay. It's fine."

"No," I was suddenly angry that he didn't try to talk to me about what had happened. I had a flash of nausea and then a pulsing headache.

"Where's my shirt?"

"Here," he said and handed it to me along with a mass of black satin. It was all I could do to hold back the tears. "Are you okay?"

"Yeah, fine." My stomach turned over and I remembered the feeling of his hand at my back.

I put my feet on the floor and the flowers on the carpet opened and pulsed. I felt dizzy, and tried to press my palms into the bed to steady myself. "I think I should go back and check on Gretchen."

"I'll walk you there."

"I'll be fine. It's just a few streets away and you need to get to work." I wanted to tell him that I had no idea how to do this. Instead I went to the bathroom and closed the door. I sat down on the floor and stared at the bathtub. I knew the set up felt familiar, I'd been there before, but allowed in Jack's gaze.

Tom knocked. "Are you coming out?" There was a tightness in the air, like taut wire. If I moved into it, a snap.

I stood up and looked in the row of mirrors over the three sinks. The blacks of my eyes were bigger than usual and that was all that had changed. Tom was at the door. I opened it and he stepped back.

"Come on," he said taking my hand and leading me down the stairs. The boy at the front grinned at us.

"The Bathers," he said in French.

"Cool art history reference," Tom said under his breath.

"Asshole," he said and made the surfer shaka symbol, bending three fingers and leaving out the pinkie and thumb on one hand.

"Were you making fun of him?" I asked confused.

"We make fun of each other. He thinks I'm some surfer kid from California."

I thought about what Jack had said to me a few weeks back. "Why is it you think choosing to be an artist makes you noble? Isn't it entitled to think you deserve that life?"

* * *

There are many fine examples of mid to late '70s films, actions, and artworks which could be labeled as avant garde. Take, as example, Dusan Makavejev's boundary pushing 1974 Sweet Movie, which gleefully skewers the European bourgeois with a sharp critique of social hypocrisy. It's an unconventional narrative, a Frankenstein of tone, a hybrid of horror-shock, pastiche, sketch comedy, and other genres. Difficult to pin down, aloof. In this twisted story, Makavejev champions of the anti-fascism of "Sexual Liberation" psychoanalyst William Reich.

One could argue a nod to Makavejev's divisive contemporaries, the musical genius of COUM and in particular, Cosey Fanni Tutti. One scene in particular mashes this all together in just a few minutes.

Welcome to the Miss World 1984 contest on an episode of "The Crazy Daisy Show." The velvet bow-tied announcer lauds it as "sophisticated entertainment" featuring the semi finalists, seven of the world's most well preserved virgins. This brouhaha is sponsored by the Chastity Belt Foundation and its chairman the matriarch, Martha Alplanalpe of the Aristotles Alplanalpe Chain Stores clan. (Family motto: "When we buy something, we buy the best and we buy it brand new.") The winner will get 50 billion dollars and become the wife of Mrs. Martha Alplanalpe's beloved son, also known as Mr. Kapital. His portrait flashes on screen, a sepia tone cowboy in front of redwoods.

The set is cobbled from a bourgeois mix of clothing and furniture (bad taste?) Mrs. Martha is wearing a long green satin sheath with a turtleneck of cool-colored pailettes, which she shakes to the beat of Bongo drums being played by three men in medieval page outfits. The stage centerpiece is an antiquated fleur de lis-painted gynecological chair that looks more like a decorative snow sledge than medical equipment.

In Fanni Tutti's memoir, she mentions an antique dealer who sold her the "wonderful Victorian dentist's chair" and its dubious provenance: a dentist who sexually abused patients under gas. That same year, Fanni Tutti was given the title Miss Gateway to Europe by Michael Scott of 11th Hour Artworks in prep for The Ministry of Antisocial Insecurity presentation as part of the Fanfare for Europe Festival in 1973. The event would also include COUM's take on the very British pageant-esque Bonny Baby Competition. Fanni Tutti would appear in a micro dress, her hair in pigtails. Cut to the end of the Sweet Movie scene, and its victor, Mademoiselle Canada. She is wearing high white snow boots with fur trim. The diamond appears again as she bends her knees in a long stretch, like an athlete in prep. Her hair in pigtails.

This scene in Sweet Movie is also essential for its decidedly bourgeois aesthetic— as seen in countless art house films of the time. Eric Rohmer is another example *of a director who makes use of such locations and interiors to subvert and explore primal desires that counter authoritarian politics.*

You may recognize some stills here.

* * *

Still October 2015, Paris

When I got back to the hotel I was still drunk. I had almost forgotten that Gretchen would be there. All I could see was an ultraviolet square projected onto her face. She was wide awake, lying in bed staring at her phone.

"He hasn't called."

"Do guys even call nowadays?"

"He's not a millennial, Mathilde," she said and flipped the light switch.

"Whoa, what happened to you?" she asked as I fell into the room.

"Long night," was all I could say before I ran to the bathroom.

"Cool, how you left me."

"I was letting you sleep," I hollered back.

I came out of the bathroom topless and sat down on the bed next to her. "You smell like box wine," she joked and then softened realizing something was wrong. She put down her phone and started to stroke my hair. "What's up?"

"I messed up," I squeezed my eyes shut.

"What happened?"

I shook my head.

"Lay down, here." She got up off the bed and pulled the covers over my shoes, to my neck. "There."

She went to the phone to call down for a bottle of water. After flailing around in her bag, she threw a hooded sweatshirt at me. I hugged it over the sheet instead of putting it on.

There was a knock at the door and a man dressed in all black appeared carrying a silver tray with a glass and bottle of water. Gretchen thanked him, took the goods and sent him away. She poured me a cup. I saw her cell light up. "Your phone..." I took the water from her and she went to check the screen.

"It's him."

"Who?"

"Christopher."

"What does he want?"

"He wants us to go out there."

"Where?"

"To this house where he is staying for his writer thing."

"Why?"

"I guess he wants us to visit."

"I feel like shit."

"I know."

"When does he want you to come?"

"Us. He wants us to go."

"When?"

"Now, I think."

"That's so him."

"Please. It might distract you…" In the sort of auto-pilot that comes from a mild hangover and knowing one pause will give way to indefinite pause, I went along. I threw on the sweatshirt and got up to change into a pair of jeans.

"I'm so grateful, Tilly." She started to pack an overnight bag.

"I need to come back and work in a little," I said making it clear I wouldn't be camping out.

"Yes, of course."

"How will we get there?"

"He called us a car."

"He did?"

"Well, no, I just called us a car."

I laughed.

Robert

Log to remember to tell Olympia

    crimson, red to read
    puns/abstraction all not definitive
     versus pictorial alphabets/ text as still life
    erotic/sexual/discursive
    objective is to defer end result
    obtain ideas of work without intention/inquiry
    then what is coded communication
    No woman touches your toe
    Makes me sad and happy at same time
    To talk to everyone is to talk to no one
    Mall grab
    Screen grab
    technopaganism
    Zozo (like the Devil but also that Japanese site that
        made a guy rich)
    don't work for my house my house works for me
    Inner Tubes
    Punk and academia
    Play on digits
    Edit and aware of the edit
    American postmodernist
    Cobra baby and elephant in Anger film
    With a number 2 Rooms 2 Go

cult of personality, make things people don't need
Renegotiating romanticism
Outside the system
Back in it
What happened to Karen Mulder?
Collects Michael Jordan
23
Boston Latin, first public school
Sense of an Ending
Reputation
It's not about cool things; it's about cool moves.
Notes in Camp
Tree
Feminist avant garde collected by misogynist.
Inversion of taste
Lack of responsibility integrity of work.
Female
Glamorous cipher-surface
Powerful female bonds
    Not currency exchange
You misunderstand me
Not pick up calls
Negative biography, what say No to
Don't access that side, live in the glamour
Short story
decisive and move on—leave and not come back
never go back
Another lost

Post agenda
Origin story
Visual and verbal wit

No one ever thinks *the* crazy thing is going to happen. Or they do, and then because they thought it, they imagine they can think it away.

Mathilde

October 2015, outside Paris

I slept the entire ride, falling silent as soon as we were outside of the city. My head hurt too much to try and think clearly through what had to be done, what had been done. I knew that a kind of unhinged hopelessness came whenever I was exhausted and I had learned to suspend real hard actionable thoughts until I'd at least gotten a little sleep.

It took about forty five minutes to get to where Christopher was staying. "This must be it," Gretchen said to the driver. I wiped my chin with the back of my hand and sat up. She was directing him to turn down an overgrown path. He complied, the stones creating a racket as they hit the bottom of the car. This continued all the way up to the house.

I had been uncertain what to expect and was surprised to find a place like the set of a Rohmer film, like those I'd watched and rewatched as an undergrad. There was a wild garden with a table half made for lunch and eight wide windows in a grid. A row of four on each floor.

We both got out of the car and stood looking up at the ivy creepers. I panned the rock wall from one window to the next. There was a glazed ceramic lamp that caught the sunspot in the second square. It was oversize, without a shade, standing next to a marble bust. Nothing but a swath of jute fabric covered the next, and then what looked like an older man crouching motionless behind another tan curtain. When I saw him it reminded me of the suspense camera pan of a documentary series. I wanted to ask Gretchen if she saw him, unsure if it was a hallucination, a side effect of my delirium. Before I could, the man pulled the length up with his hand and pushed his face against the glass. And then, let it fall and was gone.

Gretchen rang the bell, holding it down a bit too long. A lady wearing a white Peter Pan collar shirt and a black dress flung open the door. She shivered and looked from side to side, concerned to see us standing in front of her.

"Is he expecting you?"

"Christopher is," Gretchen said. The woman nodded and stepped aside so that we could see in the door. Gretchen shouldered on, which I found embarrassing. The corridor ahead was covered in wood paneling.

"Come back here," Christopher yelled. He was nowhere to be seen. I hung back with the woman and offered my hand.

"I'm Mathilde." She looked at me strangely, tilting her head as if she was considering where we'd met before. My hand became heavy in the air. Instead of offering hers, she fingered the left part of her collar and looked up the stairs as if someone might save her from engaging. "I'm sorry for my friend," I said.

"Which one?"

"I take no responsibility for Christopher." This made her smile.

"Follow me," I wandered behind her into some kind of a second kitchen. "Would you like a coffee?"

"Only if it isn't too much trouble."

"No, of course. I will bring it to you." She pointed towards the door. I kept watching her watching me.

"Are you sure?"

"Yes," she said. "Go."

I followed her direction and walked down the wood-grain hall past a painting of a smoky landscape.

"Gretchen!" I yelled.

"In here." I turned the corner into a sparse backroom with windows out into the yard. The light coming through was making faint impressions like watermarks on the blank facing wall. Gretchen's profile was clear in shadow over them. Against the opposite wall was a pale mint metal desk. Christopher was standing nearby staring at the screen of his lap top.

"Hello there, beautiful Mathilde."

"Hi Christopher."

"So, how do you two like the place?" he asked twirling around with outstretched hands.

"You have to meet the man of the house. He's legendary."

"It's a very beautiful spot. Good light."

"Did you see the library?"

"I only saw the kitchen. That lady is very nice."

"Maria's the best."

"Mila, I thought she said?"

"Same thing." He'd migrated over to the bed where Gretchen had been sitting. She got up just as he sat down on the simple cedar block base. There was a red, yellow and blue striped blanket across the bottom. "Why don't you two go walk around?" he said lying back.

"By ourselves?"

"Yeah, I just have to finish one thing." He angled his head towards his computer.

"Come," Gretchen said grabbing my hand and glaring at him. She led me down the hall. I stopped her in front of the picture. "What is it?" she asked.

"I think it's a volcano."

"I meant who is it?"

"The painter?"

"Yeah." I bent in close enough to see the impasto.

"I don't know."

"Look at that ash cloud," Gretchen made the sound of an explosion and walked into the adjacent space. It was a five sided room wallpapered in flocked green diamonds, reaching sconces jutting out from all sides. We passed through into the library.

I stepped onto the ground level rung of a ladder suspended along metal rods that ran along the top and bottom of the shelves. There were eight levels of books circling around. The ceiling was painted with faint clouds and the carpet was dark red, almost black. There was a square in the ceiling that looked like it led to a secret attic.

"What's upstairs?" I thought about the apparition from earlier.

"I don't know, but I want to go check it out."

"I might stay down here."

"Whatever you want, just don't bother Christopher. He gets weird when he's working on something."

"What is wrong with him?"

"Everything."

I laughed and ran my hand along the nearest shelf. There was a wall of philosophy. Christopher had once taken to calling me and Gretchen, Deleuze and Guattari. He had thought it hilarious. No one else had.

There was another row of editions in different languages. It took me a moment to realize they were all versions of the same title, the author's name strangely familiar.

"What is wrong with *you*?" Gretchen asked. "You look possessed." I was staring up at all the yellow spines with red serif letters.

"I've seen this book before."

"Obviously, like, in a bookstore."

"No. I know it from somewhere."

I took one off the shelf and flipped it over in my hands.

"Can I ask you something," she said.

I smiled at her usual refrain. "What's up?" I held the book to my chest and sat down cross-legged on the floor.

"Christopher said the weirdest thing earlier."

"When?"

"On the phone before."

"I thought you hadn't heard from him?"

"I forgot about this—the Klonopin."

"Go on."

"He said, 'Gretchen, I'm really fond of you, but I need to be upfront.'"

"Weird that he used the last part as like a quantifier. 'I'm really fond of you *but…*'"

"Let me finish. Anyway, so, he says, 'I need to be upfront. I'm never going anywhere and we'll always be friends. It won't change anything.'"

"What's the 'it'?"

"Us having a thing?"

"The 'thing' is an 'it.'"

"Yes."

"Continue."

"Then he said, 'So, you can let me know what you want to do.'"

She sat down next to me on the library floor. I put my hand on her leg. "He meant what he said and what he didn't say, but he didn't not say what he means. Does that make sense?"

"Not really," she said.

"He told you up front and you fell for it. He doesn't want you except when he needs entertainment. Not in a relationship, not to be responsible if you leave Sam. And he's free of blame."

As if on cue, Christopher yelled from his room. "Come back, I need your light."

I saw Gretchen blush to the compliment. "My light," she mouthed at me and got up. She ran to him. I followed behind.

"You have your stuff?" he asked when we entered.

"What stuff?"

"Your bag," He sucked down an Orangina Light and then packed a box of Marlboro Reds on the palm of his hand. "Lighter, please," he demanded. Gretchen's face fell and she rummaged through her bag pulling out a clear Bic from the Tabac. He took it and said, "I'm happy you're here, *really*.

Christopher ashed onto the floor as Mila appeared in the doorway. "Time for lunch," she said staring at me and ignoring the others. "Robert won't be joining you." Christopher looked very disappointed.

"Why?" he asked, bruised.

"I don't know," she said without making eye contact.

"I'm annoyed."

"Why?" Gretchen asked him.

"It's rude."

"He didn't invite us here, you did," she said.

"I don't care. You know what? I'm skipping lunch. I'm going to stay and work, maybe you guys can come back another time."

"You're kidding, right?"

"No."

"Why don't you two come sit in the garden. I'm sure he'll be down in a moment," Mila said turning to leave. I pulled Gretchen out of the room. I knew what was coming. I'd seen that look only once before.

Gretchen tried to go back in. The door was locked. She banged on it. "Christopher!" Metal music started playing from within.

No answer.

"Christopher!"

Still no answer, the music grew louder and louder.

"You fucking asshole!! Open the door. You can't invite people to your house and then send them away."

The music got a little louder.

Then, Gretchen started to sob. Her face contorted into a rage and then all at once, she started to cry. I put my arms around her.

"Stop, G." She was crying so hard she couldn't speak.

"Cccall the cccccar," she stuttered. I pulled out my phone and set up the taxi pickup. The address of the house populated itself via Wifi.

"Gretchen, calm down."

"He-he-he's such a fuck up. Why did I even come?"

"You came to Paris to be with me. I needed you," I said. Through the tears I saw her soften.

"I love you, Tilly."

"I love you too." No one escorted us to the door. As we walked to the driveway, I noticed the table that had been set when we pulled up was now gone.

An old Fiat arrived to pick us up. We got in without speaking and sat there in silence for most of the ride, both realizing we were powerless to prevent the other from the same things.

Robert

October 2005, Paris

For years, I had done my best to avoid anyone who needed me in service of my own work.

This is why I didn't have children. (The short list.)

And so, Olympia was perfect to chase for a while. Not always around; without need.

When our fantasy pas de deux became unbearable, I didn't consider that I wouldn't be able to fulfill her needs as a partner, only that she wasn't mine.

I wanted her to be there in my house when I woke up and when I went to sleep. She said that was the funny thing about humans, how child-like they became in the morning and at night. During the day, a suspension of dread with domestic tasks and work. It was true, I didn't want her around when I was working, and I didn't want to deal with her quotidian demands.

I wanted her, I said. And she knew the conditional reality. She was sharp, brushing me off when I tried to convince her otherwise.

Maybe eleven odd years ago, I told Olympia I'd meet her and her daughter at the Jardin des Plantes. They were in Paris together on holiday. At first she protested, but finally gave in when I made a joke about hiding behind the exotic plants, said something about banana farmers, agronomists.

I didn't show up.

Well, I was there, and I took that picture. I hid behind a wild palm and more or less paparazzi'ed the two of them, dressed alike. One of the crazier things I've ever done.

And then, I left.

Olympia didn't answer my calls or write after that. She'd managed to stage evidence of my desire for complicity and once assured, the inability to show up.

Mathilde

October 2015, Paris

My phone started buzzing, just as I settled on a bench a few blocks from the hotel. It was Tom asking if I would meet him outside at the local cafe for a drink. I started back to collect myself before answering his request.

Gretchen barreled into the lobby as I was coming in. "Where are you coming from?"

"I'm not coming, I'm going. Tom called." Her face betrayed delight.

"Because he needs something from you?"

"That's mean."

"I don't know why you don't think it's transactional?"

"It's not."

"Sex is a kind of capital."

"Please, Gretchen."

"Look at how you're dressed."

"I was going to change. What is wrong with you?"

"I'm sad. I'm sorry. I also haven't eaten in two days."

"Why don't you come with me?"

"I'm not sure he'll appreciate that."

"I'll order you something?" I took her hand and pulled her into the tiny elevator instead of taking the stairs. She shook her head. Realizing I hadn't responded, I told Tom I could leave in five minutes and asked him where to go.

"You do look really nice," Gretchen said. The door was open and the man was cleaning inside. I felt better leaving her there with the stranger.

"Thanks. I won't be too late. I promise."

"Be careful," she said.

* * *

Teddy bears or stuffed animals exist in nearly all cultures, something plush to soothe small humans. Kelley's practice often included found childhood objects, discarded crochet toys and blankets with a special interest in the transactional nature of these gifts. He blew up their images, wide-eyed stuffed animal gaze increasing its scale in print, distorted to heighten the uncanny.

Kelley also sewed together large balls of color coordinated stuffed animals, hanging the caterpillar-like creatures from strings on the ceiling. "Deodorized Central Mass with Satellites," is one rainbow soft sculpture and surrounding flea-market balls. Another project, his Arenas, features found blankets placed on the floor and matched with plush creatures.

Arena Seven is a white cloth with satin trim, a monkey at its helm, another monkey across the way. Two yellow colored koalas attached to a piece of wood sit across from a smiling pale pink bear.

Arena Five is a lonely E.T. staring across an expanse of mustard blanket to a trio of two other ET's examining a human form doll. The stuffed animals become haunting figures.

Arena Nine is subtitled (Blue Bunny) There is a tiny crocheted rabbit with a five petal flower on its belly sitting in the middle of a very big blue blanket.

A line up of strange picnics, they invite the on-looker to remember en plein air.

* * *

October 2015, Paris

Tom was already eating outside when I arrived. He was easy to find with his hooded sweatshirt and old, gray sneakers. Most of the other men at the cafe were wearing collared shirts and dress shoes. I put my hand on his back as I came around the table. He pulled away ever so slightly. I sat down across from him. There was a lit cigarette balancing in the divet on the ashtray.

"Is it okay if I get something?" I asked. He flagged down the waiter.

"I'm sorry, I was starving."

"No problem," I said and turned to the man in a red double breasted vest to order a smoked salmon plate.

"You want the toasts?" He said to me in English. "Anything else?"

"Yes and a *citron pressé*, please." He spread a paper place mat in front of me. There was already a metal tumbler of ice on the next table, which he moved within reach. "What have you been up to all day?"

"Working in the studio. And then I had this collector who's visiting from Berlin come by."

"You?"

"I went out to the country with Gretchen."

"You have family here?"

"Kind of," I don't know why I lied.

"Cool."

"Did you finish?"

"The show? I'm a long way from finishing, which is why I have to make this quick."

"Sorry?" I wasn't pleased with the tone of his voice.

He took the last sip of his beer and started, "This guy asked me to put him in touch with someone to help consign a few works, maybe he has something for you. I promised him some new paintings. Long story... Can I hook you up?"

"What?" The waiter brought a glass with thick yellow liquid and a carafe of water. Tom poured them together, adding more and more until the lemon juice was the palest version of its original concentrate.

He handed me the drink. "I just mentioned that one of my collectors has a few works he wants to consign." I tried to muster a fake smile. "You're a funny girl," he said with affection. "And super beautiful."

Despite this last part, I was annoyed. I pushed back a little from the table and tried to cross my legs so he would see my stockings. "You could have emailed me?" He laughed uncomfortably.

"I thought it would be nice to see one another." He looked at the ground and gave a limp smile. "I'm going to have to get going." He pulled a fifty euro bill out of his pocket. "I'm sorry I have to run. We'll catch up soon?" I was unable to speak, afraid to show my disappointment. "Bye, Mathilde." I waved my hand. He left me there alone with the salmon. I took a bite and tugged at the ankle of my tights.

I ate quickly, hoping the toast would mop my uneasy stomach.

On any other evening, I would have texted Gretchen to relay the events and ask for her analysis. Doing so would have given her great satisfaction and despite knowing that she could use a little buzz, I kept Tom's ghost of a dinner to myself.

After asking the waiter after the bill, (Tom had taken care of it) I walked around the neighborhood for an hour, peering into the familiar windows. Both the lingerie and toy shop were dark, their dressings works in progress. It had once again started to rain.

It took ten minutes for me to get back to the hotel. The woman at the front desk offered a towel and told me that Gretchen had gone out. I took the stairs and counted them all the way to the fourth floor.

The room was neat and silent. I sat on the bed cross legged and opened my computer. Tom had already sent the introduction over email. It was equally as late in Berlin as it was in Paris, so I decided to wait until the morning to call. I turned my attention to his email going over every word for hidden meaning.

I closed the computer, undressed and carefully lay my clothes on the tufted chair next to the bed. The now brown flower fell onto the floor, like crumbs caught after dinner in the fold of a dress. It left an indentation where it had been held in nylon, pressed too tightly into salty skin. I could make out the head of the fallen daisy when I examined the spot, pulling it taut with two fingers. A light was turned on in a room across the courtyard. I saw it through the mirror, a bright point in my reflection.

Fuck him.

I tried to think about anything else. Ruminating on Tom's behavior was a way to avoid confronting my own. If I became unduly righteous and cut him off, I wouldn't have anything to offer Charles. I realized by this analysis alone, I was playing into the unregulated game between men and artwork, romance between buyer to seller-seller to buyer. Like any advertising to make one want the thing that could make life breezier, better. The onlooker's hot take is rooted in naiveté about the calculated alchemy of her seduction.

The only comfort I could manufacture was that Jack was someone who had nothing to do with any of this. And he would disappear if I bought too far in. Maybe he was already gone.

Two to four years and they say the "in love" feeling wears off, the chemicals change. The only way to keep it is to restart every time it ends. If you want the chemical high you need to come up with a schedule. Be a serial wife. Gretchen and her theories about love and addiction. You can have theories though and not follow them. Scientists among us.

At midnight, as if on schedule, Gretchen knocked on the door.

"Tilly, let me in!"

"Hold on. I'm coming." I had fallen asleep for fifteen minutes on top of the covers without any clothes on. Pulling her sweatshirt over my head, I opened the door. She laughed at my face poking through the neck hole before I was able to pull the shoulders down.

"My phone died. Thank g-d you're not asleep."

"I wish."

"What's wrong?" She threw her bag down and climbed into bed. I closed the door and turned on the light. Her hand flew to her eyes. "Too bright," she moaned.

"You're not going to change into different clothes?"

"I didn't really do anything. I just went to have a few beers by the river."

"By yourself?"

"Yeah," she shrugged.

"I don't believe you." She smiled.

"And I don't believe you." I still hadn't told her what she knew about me and Tom.

"I want to be in love," I said in defense.

"Are you twelve?"

I climbed into bed next to her. She moved away. I saw a flicker of annoyance when my feet touched hers and knew she was about to say something she'd been trying not to.

"You're too dumb or self-obsessed or something to see you have what everyone wants and I underline that with I don't give a fuck what anyone wants."

"You're wasted." I could smell the alcohol on her. "Don't act like you've cultivated this off center cool. You were born into extreme privilege. It's that which allows you not to care." It took only a minute and we were aiming exactly where we knew would cause the other the most hurt.

Gretchen inched over further to the other side of the bed. "What I was born into was a mess that you're about to make. My father fucked around his whole life, one woman to the next. No responsibility. He would fall out of love and then withdraw and take up with the next receptive candidate. And then he died. I was the only one who cared, and out of obligation."

"Be careful. You're drunk."

"You're a selfish, little cunt."

"Gretchen."

"You want this high from the attention, and the crazy passion, but it comes with fall out. It's like sleeping pills. It would be different if you were an eighteen year old girl, but you're nearly thirty. You no longer have the luxury of being a neurotic romantic."

"You do somehow?"

"You made a decision, which is the only thing that allows you to even entertain these fantasies. You want the complexity and drama and torture to validate your existence, but what if it negates it, chipping away at your reality for what doesn't even exist. Have you heard from Tom since that night?"

"What if what validates your reality is that you are grounded and committed, invested in something?" She didn't want an answer. "You have that. And still, you seek the poser that's going to claim he loves you; to crush on you, because that's what it is. He doesn't know Mathilde, only the doll. I, on the other hand, love you, but acknowledge you're fucked up; not at all a doll. Jack knows this too, and he's fine with it," Gretchen pulled herself out of bed to use the bathroom. She turned to look at me. "I don't look for stability where I get my passion."

"That was the most profound thing you've ever said."

"Least profound, really." She closed the door and threw up.

* * *

The next day, Christopher had a bouquet of peonies delivered to the hotel.

The card read: "To brighten your day."

Not "Love, Christopher," as he'd written in the past.

A gesture inverted with the withholding of words. He did it to destabilize Gretchen. It was a skill to answer someone with a few characters and sentences of subtext. There are men who get off on appearing the good guy while behaving badly.

"How dare he!" she said aloud after the bell boy left. His buzzing with the delivery had woken both of us up.

"Calm down."

"He can't just do that. I fucking slept with him."

"He can do whatever he wants. That's what he does," I said.

"It's illogical though. There's no consistency."

"He's consistently inconsistent."

"Fair." I grabbed the bouquet of flowers en route to the bathroom and started tearing off their heads, tossing them into the toilet. "What are you doing?"

"Decapitating your flowers."

"Fuck off," she said. "My head hurts so much."

"Hold on, I'm coming." I presented her with two Tylenol and a glass of water.

"You know I love you." There was a low buzz coming from somewhere in the room. I got down on all fours to search the floor next to the bed for a phone. "It's over there by the bathtub," Gretchen said.

"Where? I don't know what you're talking about."

She sat up and swallowed, then growled in frustration and nearly fell out of the bed on her way to the bathroom. "Oh wait, it's mine," she said. I heard running pipes. She stuck her head out. "The toilet's clogged, because you flushed half my flowers down it." I heard a thumping and a clink, her phone vibrated and jumped the rim.

"Oh. Shit"

"Did it crack?"

"No, but he texted."

"What did he say?" I asked.

"That he wants us to come back and meet that guy…"

"Fuck that."

"Please, Tilly. *Please*. You know how much this would mean to me."

"He sucks. I can't reason with you anymore."

"How is your situation any different?"

"Tom hasn't treated me like that."

"Christopher is a genius. This is how he works."

"Oh, like the time he told you he's more or less a Marvel superhero that needs a man-servant-butler type around for company. Time spent with his lover though, must be erratic."

"Not unlike you."

"I'm not going. That place creeps me out."

"Let's revisit in an hour," she said pushing the phone under her pillow. "I need to lie back down."

PART III:
WAYS OF FLEEING

Mathilde

"Hi, may I please speak with Mr. Linek," I asked the woman on the other end of the office landline. She had answered in German. I didn't understand and felt badly assuming English. There was silence and then a man's voice with a strained accent.

"Mathilde?"

"This is she."

"I'm happy you called. Tom told me you would been in touch."

"Forgive me, if this is a bad time." I looked across the room to the round mirror hung parallel to the bed on top of a maze of red velour. I crossed my legs in the opposite direction. The left leg over the right one, the reverse shown to me. Gretchen was a tan lumpen thing. My eyes looked heavy, my hair a mess. I switched the phone to speaker and held it to my chin and with the other hand put my second and fourth fingers on my eyes and turned my head away in tired shame.

"Would you be able to hop on a plane over here? I'd like to show you a few things." His voice came out loud and clear, startling me. Gretchen didn't move. I sat up and pushed my shoulders back. He didn't bother with pleasantries or the option of refusal. "I'll have my assistant secure it for you. Could you head to the airport around this time tomorrow if not right now?"

Jack would have argued that a pause would only have been a gain. "I can go right now," I said smashing my eyes closed, embarrassed at my eagerness.

"That works. I'll have her send you all the details. Head to Le Bourget."

All that and Gretchen was still sleeping. There was a strange pallor to her skin in the morning light and I reached over to feel if she was breathing. She was. It was the hundredth time I'd done that.

I fished through my purse to see if I had any cash to leave. I found fifty euros and stuck it in an envelope on the drawbridge desk. It was a lot, but all I had, and fitting to clean up the mess we had left the night before.

And I knew I would return in less than a day and see the same faces. The ones that knew us and our indiscretions. Realized or not, they were in the stale air and someone would have to take them out.

I didn't bother brushing my hair or changing from the old jeans and gray sweater. After patting my head, I pulled the nest back into a high ponytail, tying it with a black ribbon I pulled off the handle of one of the shopping bags. Having run out of socks, I was still wearing tights covered in a grid strung together by black dots. The French word for them was "pois." Like tiny peas. The layers made my jeans fit tighter than usual and I felt a little uncomfortable.

I threw my high Mary Janes into the back of the tiny closet and instead chose black mid height boots that once belonged to my mother. She'd had a few pairs of them. It was strange to take someone's shoes, but we were the same size. I had always admired them. They weren't obviously sexy or glamorous.

Gretchen still hadn't stirred and I decided not to wake her. It was unclear if I would make it even if I left at that very moment. I took the orange Clairefontaine notebook I'd brought off the window ledge and tried to wedge it into my handbag. The edges bent forward and the card stock back cover gave way tulipping down. I'd have to try calling Gretchen in the car or leave word for her at the front desk.

The room phone rang and startled me, but the taxi I had called came up as an alert on my cell, and I decided to let whoever it was leave a message. Gretchen didn't move. I watched her chest lift and fall before stepping lightly backwards out of the room. Holding my bag in the air, I ran down the stairs two at a time.

"Madame," the boy at the front started. I waved at him, which he took as a quieting. So, he waved back at me before writing something down behind the desk. I wanted to stop but I could see the car stalling out front with its passenger seat window rolled down to show the driver throwing his face forward like a turtle. He tutted when I got in the car. I settled into the back seat and ignored his hooded eyes wanting to be met through the rearview mirror.

Instead, I watched through the back window as the distance between buildings got wider. I tried calling Gretchen's phone to leave a message. Straight to voicemail. It must have run out of batteries, sitting there on the edge of the bathroom sink.

I kept thinking I should call Jack and ask his advice on everything. It was strange that I couldn't. He had become a kind of stand in for parents, which is a lot when you are also partner and lover.

Because of him, I was able to be half that for someone else.

I once overheard my mother sitting with a friend in the kitchen. She rarely had friends over and most often they weren't other women, but something had happened. I don't know what. She sat there drinking tea across from Dorothy who was still wearing her scrubs from the hospital.

I'd known Dorothy since as long as I could remember. She worked at the local emergency room, which is why I thought she was never around. They were talking in hushed voices. My mother said something about "all-in intimacy" being required for a life partner, that this was "nonsense, a construct of the patriarchy." I hadn't known what any of that meant. Dorothy had agreed.

"To keep you in check, to know what you're up to," she'd said. She'd also said that she was looking for a rationalization, "the hallmark of delinquency." My mother had shot back something about intention and loyalty. All the big words had confused me, but I remember a full sentence of what she said at the end. She had pushed her tea cup away and folded her hands on the table. "The going away game is always about the departed."

The scene out the window had become strips of blue gray on green. No more buildings or tunnels. I thought about how I wanted to distance myself from the last few days. And at the same time, felt contempt for my younger self, the earlier woman who had led me here, and anyone who had loved her. I could cut ties, but she wouldn't go.

I was moving as fast as I could so that if I took aim, I'd miss. Calling Linek and running to meet him meant that I was keeping Tom in play. Allowing the favor was consummating another exchange.

Still Mathilde

October 2015, Berlin

I was worried I wouldn't be able to find Linek's driver when I got off the plane, but it was a tiny receiving area of the private airport. The man was easy to identify, standing there, wearing a corduroy blazer and acid washed jeans. He nodded at me, the only young woman in sight, as I passed the glass transom. He offered to take my bag and I refused, following behind him to a black Mercedes waiting, running, parked at the curb. Three policemen walked by, glanced at the car's plates and walked on. He opened the door and I climbed in. I'd slept the short plane ride and was still coming out of it. He gave me a questioning glance and I assured him that I had everything.

I tried Gretchen again. Straight to voicemail. If she didn't reach out in an hour, I would call the hotel to check on her. Jack had left a message while I was on the plane. I read the transcription. It was empty. I knew what he had to say, something like "Hey Mati, Calling to see how you're doing. Talk to you in a bit." Simply the missed call told me this, which was good as I didn't want to hear his voice. It was funny how unlike a young relationship it was, without the wasted hours of discussion and decoding that came with every new exchange.

It felt as if I was back in the cab from the hotel, head pushed up against the window watching, except the buildings multiplied. Berlin came closer, the lines of open landscape shortened and the shapes piled up. The driver looked back at me in the rearview mirror and said, "Five more minutes," as if I had asked for an ETA. His phone rang and he said something in German and hung up. "Change of plan. Mister wants you to go to his house." I hadn't realized there had been any other agenda. I looked away pretending to search for something in my bag. Within minutes, we'd pulled onto a street with a large bunker-like stone house made of curved igloo lines. There was a man dressed in jeans, a navy sweater, and track shoes standing outside. He waved the driver forward. We pulled up and he opened the door on my side.

"Hello, I'm Joerg," he said extending his arm. He had long hair and wore dark brown glasses.

"Pleasure," I said taking his hand with one hand and adjusting the back of my sweater with the other, as I climbed out of the car.

"I hope the flight was fine. It is kind of you to come all this way, and I know you had business in Paris."

"It's really not that far." The sky had darkened a little since I'd landed. Again, rain.

"It wasn't part of your original plan."

"It was kind of Tom to put us in touch."

"Yes, I hadn't been looking to consign anything, but he kept speaking about this extraordinary young woman who he thought I should meet. I'm not usually down with this." It sounded like he was trying out a phrase he'd heard somewhere. I was careful not to laugh.

"That is kind. I've always wanted to meet you, have heard so much about your collection and the programming you support." He smiled and led me into the house.

It was even colder inside the strange stone palace. Linek saw me shiver and offered to get me a sweater. I agreed. He left me alone in the entryway, an empty platform landing. I could see into the gray-painted hallway. Three different sized Berber rugs of white and black diamonds were on the floor like woven lily pads over the concrete. "Do come in," he yelled without looking back. I followed the yarn squares through the corridor into an even larger room. There was no furniture except for a table with a pale mint green metal base on compass legs and a thick slab of wood on top. The walls were filled with large scale works, two on each SUV-sized surface. They weren't conventional walls, four to a space. This room had seven, and an equal number of squares cut in the ceiling letting the sky in. At that moment, the whole place was covered in the palest all over shadow from the overcast day. No shapes cast on the floor; no objects to block the light. "Would you like a tour?" he asked offering me a neon red turtleneck. I didn't really want it or his show and tell.

"Yes, please." I followed him through another corridor, this one carpeted floor to ceiling in tan plush. As we walked through, he ran his hand along the soft wall. We came to another large open space with a folding screen cutting it in two. "That's a funny choice," I said.

"It's only temporary. I needed a few more walls."

"Oh." Linek came from a long line of art collectors. In an effort to distance himself from them, so he could effectively become one of them, he had decided to pursue a career as an academic. Sometimes he also pretended he was a writer hyphenate and wrote more accessible pop culture commentary. One of his essays had appeared in a news magazine Jack had been reading a few months ago. I had noticed the name "Linek" on the cover and when he put the magazine down—he always read them cover to cover—I asked if I could have a look.

The essay was illustrated with a Cy Twombly painting on the first page, and one of Tom's works on the second. I couldn't remember exactly which ones. The piece was about Linek's interest in the overlap and play between the visual and literary arts. Tom's work circumvented the given boundaries, which is why Linek had taken such an intent and early interest.

"Would you like a drink?" he asked.

"Tequila, please." I wondered where he'd get the glass. Someone appeared from nowhere with a bottle in hand, cup and a kind of small popup folding table. I looked away and then back and there appeared an urn shaped clear vase filled with white flowers, like a film set. And then, two chairs. Linek sat down in one. Another woman came in and handed him a bottle of beer.

"So, I may want to unload a few works. As you know, I have a large collection of Tom's paintings. I was fascinated from the first time I went to his studio and saw his process. At that moment, I was heavy into Michaux," he paused to take a drink. "Would you be interested?"

I felt kind of ill. I thought maybe it was the lighting or the aftermath of all that other drinking. Or maybe his put on voice echoing in the concrete room.

"Yes, of course. Thank you."

The London office was smaller, more intimate than our New York heart. It was only three floors each with a large conference center and three satellite rooms. There was always a silver box for our umbrellas and cupboards to hang our coats. We liked to watch each other rearrange the desks.

It had been difficult for Alice to decide where to place the horn ornament she'd gotten on vacation with her boyfriend in Morocco. The one, she'd met when she was studying abroad at Oxford from her university in Miami, Florida.

They'd visited the souk every day after having a pot of mint green tea. Alice would request hers without sugar. It had been a beautiful trip.

She'd bought so many djellabas that she got stopped at customs.

It took fifteen minutes for the Oxford-educated Alice to decide that placing the horn to the left of the stack of books was more aesthetically pleasing. She then decided to arrange the books on the shelves by spine color, in descending rainbow order.

That's Purple first. Not Red.

She didn't have a blue one, though, which threw everything off. And her pens were not quite right. She had found three of those sort of giveaway plastic ones from restaurants she'd never heard of, which she hid out of sight in Mathilde's desk drawer. Then, she sat back in the mid-century modern chair her father had given her when she got the job and admired her handiwork. She flattened the skirt of her dress with her palms and turned to look at the rest of us.

"Where is Mathilde?"

"She's in Berlin, I think. My friend who works for a gallery there said there was a rumor she'd gone to see Joerg Linek."

"You can't be serious?"

"She sounded fairly certain, knows someone who works for him as a PA. Talked to her on the phone. I, for one, don't know for certain, but I think they may have hooked up. You know how it is with Mathilde; this beautiful nymph comes to visit, all quirky and disarming."

"Do you think we should mention this to Charles?"

"How?"

"Like, he should know."

"Poor Jack."

"Everyone knows."

"She sleeps with all the clients."

"I nominate Alice to address it."

"I don't know."

"No one likes her. I even asked that little intern, 'Are you friends with Mathilde?' She looked all scared and shook her head."

"When have you ever spoken to the interns?"

"It was just that one time."

"Charles left his email open yesterday."

"Did you look?"

"His assistant always has access."

"This was his personal email."

"I saw a note he had started to write to her."

"Who?"

"Mathilde."

"What do you mean?"

"I don't know, but seemed suspect."

"Everything about her is suspect."

"Him."

"No, her."

"I think you should look more closely next time."

"Nah."

"Why not?"

"Karma."

"Lol," someone said out loud.

Mathilde

October 2015, Berlin

Linek had tried to insist that I stay the night in Berlin, but I wanted to get back for Gretchen. I hadn't heard from her, no proof of life online or off. And I couldn't bare to be in that dark, cold house any longer. The artwork wasn't exciting. It felt like someone had stolen all the originals, replaced them with graying replicas. Or a fire safety faucet had gone off coating all the canvases with dirty water even if it was only dirty sunlight. During my tour, I'd been shown the entire ground floor, all thirteen rooms of nothing but wall space. Linek told me he slept upstairs, but I never saw signs of a personal life.

I was being suffocated even though there was nothing around me.

As a parting gift, Linek had given me a copy of a few Berger books, which was both reductive and insulting. The collection of his shorter pieces on artist lives was a beautiful brick of a thing that only made me want to escape faster.

Linek sensed my discomfort and suggested we take a walk outside. I assured him that I was fine and would call a car to take me to the airport even if it meant waiting alone while the details were sorted. I felt useless and unlucky to be so lucky.

I was part of a system that would allow me to take a cut for showing up to the right address, being pleasant enough, and then handling some very basic logistics. I couldn't really mess it up if I tried. This proved, however, not to be true.

"Leave me all your information: Address, Phone number etc. Write it here on this paper," Linek waved a white sheet in the air. "I will pass it along to Marie."

"Oh, I had called her Margot, by accident. I thought she had said—."

He stopped me, "No, you were correct. Margot is the woman you spoke to before. She is leaving me on Monday. Wants to be a singer."

He said it like it was the most natural thing in the world.

Margot had been stellar at aiding my escape. She'd made one phone call and screamed something in German. By then, my cab had shown up to take me to the airport. I'd procrastinated filling out the blank sheet Linek had given me until the very last minute. She'd watched me with an uncertain expression as I wrote down an email and phone number and finally, an address. I've always been a shitty actress. This first act made me worry about what would happen when I was finally in front of Jack. Act I Part IV.

The ride to the airport was the same as the one out of Paris. And the short hop back was just as uneventful as the nap I'd taken on the way over. I was worried about Gretchen. It had been too long to not be.

Still Mathilde

October 2015, Le Bourget airport en route to Paris

As soon as we landed, I turned my phone off airplane mode and there were multiple pop up messages.

"Please answer me. What do I do?" And then another follow up in the same color bubble:

"He wrote, 'I'm sorry; I love you.' He texted me. I didn't text him, I swear." Gretchen was back.

I started to type and then stopped myself, deleted, "He's playing you." She wanted consolation, kindness, not a reinstatement of the obvious. She had seen the three moving gray dots and fired off another message.

"He's playing me."

I wrote back as gently as I could: "He will always rationalize his faults as eccentricities." The phone rang. I'd written the right, enabled thing.

"Tilly, I need you," Gretchen said.

"I was in Berlin, working. You know that."

"I went to see him."

"I thought you said you didn't text him?"

"I didn't; I went to see him and then later he texted."

"Gretchen. When are you going to stop allowing this. It's like he's the one person who can do whatever he wants and you'll accept it. Everyone else is always getting cast out."

"Not you."

"Right. Our stellar dynamic."

"When are you back?"

"It will probably take me about an hour to get there. I'm at the airport."

"Okay," she said and hung up the phone.

I checked my email to see if Tom had gotten in touch. He hadn't.

The traffic from the airport was unusual. The last time I had been to Berlin was with Jack, three years ago. I didn't know why I'd forgotten that until I'd accomplished the trip. It was as if I could only process so much without adding in more story. On the ride back to the hotel, I thought about having gone with him to a summit of some kind. I couldn't remember the specifics, only how I'd left.

After being alone in a hotel for much of the trip, I'd gotten frustrated. It wasn't out of neglect or his relentless schedule. Despite the pressure, he'd been calm and attentive, checking in at every break. Sometimes when he called, I wouldn't pick up. He'd text me afterward, telling me he had tried and would see me later. And I'd still get frustrated. And he remained patient through my tantrums. Every time. The breakdowns always played out the same way:

"What's wrong Mati?" I would be sitting on the floor in the bathroom of the hotel with my head down.

"Nothing," I'd yell back.

He'd walk over and I would refuse to look at him.

"I'm not sure how much more of this I can take," he'd say and I'd look up.

"Jack, something just doesn't feel right."

"What does that even mean?"

"I don't know."

"I think we have it pretty good. There's something off about your desire to have things feel right. It's allowing yourself to gauge your life on a mood." It was the only time I had ever seen him look really upset. His thick eyebrows had gone up and those steady blue eyes had stared at me for longer than felt comfortable. I'd played back with a coy downward glance. I'd picked a tissue out of the box and started to tear it to little pieces on the floor. He had looked like he was about to tear it out of my hand or hit me. Of course, he did neither.

"You are so out of touch with any emotion. Not everything is political."

"You're not a lesser human for being engaged in what is." He just stood there looking at me as if he was making a decision, not a simple choice, but a life-altering one.

"Stop doing that!"

"What?" He had put his right hand behind his neck, folded down his collar and started to roll his head like one does when he has a backache.

"I don't know, Jack." These cracks of mine had become common. The last two had happened in Bucharest and Munich and then before that, back in New York. "Why?" I asked as he finally lost patience and started to walk away.

"What?"

"Why do you put up with this?"

"Because I love you." He rarely said those words and made a point to do so never in defense or asking forgiveness. "Then it's a manipulation," he'd once explained when listening to the latest saga from Gretchen.

I'd shot back: "You're in private now, Jack. You don't need to be so diplomatic."

Robert

October 2015, outside Paris

I tried my best to work. It was difficult to concentrate. Every few hours when I heard a sound, I would get up from my desk and pull back the tan curtain to see who had arrived. It was always just the wind or a delivery man.

Mathilde

October 2015, Paris

It was so late when I arrived back to the hotel that the front doors were closed. Two enormous rust-colored steel walls that met together with a visible sliding lock. I rang the bell, pushing the tiny gold button, squinting to see it in the dark. The air was cold and unlike in Berlin, dry, and the sky clear. No one was answering.

I walked to the edge of the street and looked up trying to see in the window of my room. It was glowing and I was certain that Gretchen was there. I buzzed again.

A new boy, one I'd never met before, parted the doors. His head came through backlit so that it was a circle with a coil of thick hair. "Mademoiselle?" he said. They usually called me "Madame." It rang like a judgment.

"Yes?"

"Well, first come in," he said stepping back, letting the sliver in show the transom towards the stairs. "I am sorry to ask you this, but I don't think your friend is well." His English wasn't very good.

"What do you mean?"

"Well, she came done to smoke a cigarette at the beginning of my shift and looked quite bad."

"Where is she now?" He pointed upward. I left him there jabbing his finger in the air and ran up the stairs.

The door was open a crack and I saw in: the bed unmade, half-eaten food everywhere. I found Gretchen collapsed sideways on the bathroom floor, ashen colored, her loafers still half-on.

"Gretchen!" I shook her and touched her face. Her eyes opened.

"Please don't be so dramatic, Tilly. I feel sick."

"What happened?"

"I don't know. Christopher came over and we fought and drank and fought and I don't remember."

"I thought you went to see him?"

"Yes, well, at the museum where he was spending the afternoon. This was after I told him he was a liar and that he needed to never speak to me again."

I pulled her up off the floor to the sink. She resisted for only a moment and then went along. I ran the faucet and splash-tested the water and threw some on her face, and then, on my own.

I had to catch myself before telling her that she was becoming one of the girls she hated. She'd spent so much on Christopher that she'd stopped doing anything of her own. Slowly, she was morphing once again into that artist-adjacent co-opting the creativity and access of her sexual partner.

I held back less to protect her, and more to protect myself. I knew she would counter that I was side-stepping creating anything at all. We would slip back into the insult banter of our unconditional-conditional love.

"I have ideas," Gretchen said defensively as if she was reading my mind.

"Have you?"

"Fuck you."

"Don't spend another moment on him then. You like that he doesn't give you what you want. You've always gotten what you want." She didn't argue. "He's not going to end it. He's just going to keep coming back when he senses you're almost gone."

"What do I do?"

"You do nothing. You quit. You depart."

"What are you doing?" I had started to pack up my things, rolling up the stockings thrown over the chair. "You just got back. It's almost three a.m."

"I have to leave tomorrow morning to go to London. You know that."

"I'm coming with you."

"I have to work."

"Whatever that means."

"Have you seen my other gray sweater?"

"No."

"Weird. I can't find it." I scavenged through the piles of papers and new museum books Gretchen had stacked on the floor. "What's this?" I asked holding up an envelope with my name on it.

"Oh, shit. I forgot. That's for you from Christopher. He made me promise not to open it. I've been dying to."

"I can't believe you didn't."

"I couldn't risk it. He would know and use it against me."

"Even the way you think about him is abusive."

I tore open the envelope. Inside was a sheet stamped with Kodak stock logo. I turned it over. The other side was a photograph with orange robot digits at the lower right, code for a day almost a decade ago. There were two women dressed in similar clothes, one smiling, the other looking off past the camera.

I held it up to show Gretchen.

"Holy shit." She grabbed it from me and held it up close to her face. "Is that you? I lost my right contact earlier."

"Yes and my mother," I grabbed it back.

"Why did Christopher have that?"

"Did he say anything else before he gave it to you?"

"Only that he'd found it in some desk at that house."

It was all I could handle to get everything packed, including Gretchen, to the Eurostar in time to make the train we'd gotten tickets for. We'd both passed out mid conversation four hours before the wake up call came from the boy. I was startled out of a deep sleep by the bleating phone and still had to shake Gretchen to get her to open her eyes.

As soon as we were up and stumbling around, trying to cobble all of our things together, I'd pulled out the photograph from where I'd stored it in the wooden desk to make sure it was there.

My mother had been caught looking just off, but I was staring straight ahead. Strange to have your younger self staring at you. I tried to remember at that moment, who was on the other side of the camera. My hair was in a ponytail with a black ribbon. It was the same brown as my mother, which she wore tousled, half pushed back behind her shoulders. We were dressed exactly alike in matching gray sweaters. I laid the picture down on top of the book I'd taken from the house, paused, and then, tucked it inside the front cover and put the whole thing in my bag.

I had to sit on my suitcase to lock its hatches. The purchases I'd made in Paris were enough to make the difference. Gretchen, as usual, had no trouble with her luggage as she didn't have any. She'd thrown everything into three cardboard boxes, which she'd sealed with packing tape and given to the boy to DHL back to Sam's studio. I'd asked her what she planned to wear in London. She argued that she wouldn't stay long.

She'd known not to ask too much about the photo, to just meet in quiet recognition that Christopher's Robert was my Robert.

For me, the picture was only confirmation. For her, the revelation.

This man was alive and in the world. It was only inevitable that we would find each other. For years, I thought he would reach out, try to see me, find me. He never had.

I'd found him.

He'd done nothing.
I'd become good at doing nothing too.
No.
Yes.
He had found me.

* * *

*Nouveau roman writer, former banana farmer Robbe
Grillet uses descriptions of objects and space as simply
that. "What I find extraordinary is the actual presence
of this opaque world," he says and writes objects in
their barest way, existing in space.*

*When Roland Barthes wrote about his friend
Robbe Grillet, he makes mention of those that paint
still life with sheen, as "an attempt to endow its object
with an adjectival skin." This is not Robbe Grillet; he
doesn't want what's seen overridden with sensation.
He's not complicating meaning with layers, the mere
existence of a physical thing remains extraordinary.
"(His) description of an object finds its analogies with
modern painting (in its broadest acception), for the
latter has abandoned the qualification of space by
substance in favor of a simultaneous "reading" of the
planes and perspectives of its subject, thereby restoring
the object to its "essential bareness."*

*Robbe Grillet's fellow nouveau romanian Duras
is an example of a writer who defied boundaries of*

genre, writing from her own life. She was experimental in her work, interested in distilling sentences, in aisles of meaning, creating visual images with words, but at the same time, what was not said. The last chapter of Duras' book Writing *is titled "The Painting Exhibition." She writes, "We leave him to his misfortune, to that infernal obligation that outstrips any commentary, any metaphor..."*

Duras creates pictures as ciphers, ingress to complicated thoughts and drives.

Mathilde

November 2015, London

It was a bad idea to take Gretchen to the office, but I had to stop in. Charles had called some sort of meeting. I only knew, because I obsessed over refreshing my email, waiting for a divine rite that would explain what to do next.

All of the girls already knew who Gretchen was out of reverse human interest. She was a totem for what happens when a girl makes the wrong choices. No commercial organization or fancy institution at her back, and only a best friend who's an outcast.

Why they took interest in Gretchen to begin with was because she was born into her own kind of establishment. Moored to a family legacy, one that was public and known. It gave them great delight to watch her whenever they could, either through gossip or media, never first hand until that moment.

All four of them swiveled their heads when we came into the room, like robots they paused cocked to the left.

"This is Gretchen," I announced.

"Nice to meet you," they said, though it sounded like "We know."

Gretchen shook her head and went wandering in the hall, leaving me with the girls.

I sat down at the desk I always used when I was there.

Colored pencils in yellows and pale pinks were scattered on top and in the drawer, crumbled up Ryman receipts next to a pile of hotel and restaurant pens. Eventually, someone would do an expense report. I straightened and paper-clipped them and put all the pencils face up in a silver cup. The girls pretended to be busy sending links of things to buy to one another.

"Where did your friend go?"

"She had to use the rest room."

"It's been a long time."

"I should probably go check on her."

"You should. You should. You should." They all bobbed and nodded.

* * *

Marcel Broodthaers Décor: A Conquest, was the 1974 inaugural exhibition for the Institute of Contemporary Art in London.

Decor is French for both scenery and stage set. Mallarme wrote, "La Decoration! Tout est dans ce mot," which roughly translates as "Decoration! everything is in that word." An acknowledgement only half earnest. The exclamation point its giveaway.

This show featured two installation rooms, XIXth Century and XXth Century.

Salle XIXe Siecle: Two cannons on squares of Astroturf facing a taxidermies python, its tail coiled in a counter clockwise spiral, its head rearing cobra-like. More patches of grass with potted house plants or two wooden chairs upholstered in red velvet. A side table with twisted candelabra. Another with a pair of spouted wooden barrels overhead hangs a Western film still. A firearm resting on a white display cube. Set lights illuminated the staging of two red crustaceans playing cards. The lobster sits across from the crab, piles of cards, a ten of hearts and king of diamonds face up between them.

Salle XXe Siecle: A patio set with umbrella and four chairs with blue striped cushions. Two sets of shelves hold a display of fake guns. There are two benches and a jigsaw puzzle of the Battle of Waterloo on the table.

Broodthaers would have bristled at calling this an installation. It stands in as the set for an accompanying film, The Battle of Waterloo.

Everything has its place within a place.

Broodthaers was a poet until age forty when he decided to go straight up artist.

* * *

"Another day, another hotel room bed with you," I said to Gretchen, before tucking her into the cream-colored sheets.

"You wouldn't have it any other way," she said laughing. "I like this place." She ran her hand along the pink and yellow pastoral comforter.

"You love kitsch."

"I love English country. Look at that print, ugh. Neander-toile."

"Not funny. Kitsch. Go to bed."

"Where are you going?"

"I have to meet Charles. We left before he arrived at the office."

"I'm exhausted."

"Close your eyes."

"Why are you always tidying up everything?"

If I paused for too long, I'd be paralyzed. For now, I had to meet Charles and dress to his liking.

"What should I wear?"

"You look cool, Mathilde," he'd always say whenever he saw me, as if it surprised him.

"Not your gray sweater."

I pulled on a denim shirt and a pair of tight fitting jeans. Charles would inevitably comment on the outfit. He'd stare past me and speak as if he was reading cue cards off in the distance, doling out compliments like bait awaiting reflexive take. He never gave them for free.

I pulled my hair up into a knot and shivered remembering what it had felt like when my mother had done the same. "Gretchen, I have to run out. You'll be okay?" I knew she wasn't sleeping.

"Yeah," she said, her eyes closed, a lace trimmed pillow held over her head.

I shut the door gently and took the elevator down to street level. I was careful to watch for cars coming the other way. This strained awareness reminded me of being in London right after college. The street was a few down from where I'd gone to school. Jack had been new and so had this city.

The bar where Charles wanted to meet was only a few minutes away. When I walked in, the bartender motioned towards a black stool. I sat down across from the window where light was falling in slats on the beverage levers, and watched the man behind the counter lift a green handle. The bright rectangle rose onto his hand. Charles walked in. He saw me, waved, then came over and bent low for a kiss.

I gave him my right cheek and then we switched to the other side.

"We'll have two, please. Beer is fine, Mathilde?"

"For sure."

"So, how'd it go in Berlin?"

"He was really gracious. Nice. Easy."

"Did you approach him?"

"Who?"

"Joerg."

"Oh," I was surprised. I thought he knew the story.

"Oh no, it was Tom that put us in touch."

Charles raised his eyebrows. "That's quite an extraordinary favor," he said searching my face, looking through me. I turned around to see if anyone was there.

"It was kind of him."

"How is your life, Mathilde? No, really," he insisted.

"I'm not sure what you mean."

"I'm worried about you." I uncrossed my legs and recrossed them.

"I'm fine. Really. Just working quite hard." I looked up at him and knew he was intimating that I was having trouble at home.

"How did you fall in with Tom?" It took me a moment to realize what he'd actually asked.

"We've known each other through going out for sometime."

"I see." I wasn't sure how to react to this new tone. I hated when people make a point to respond with that strange rhetorical, "I see." It's the flip side of asking "Can I ask you a question?"

I wanted to explain to him that it was a platonic friendship, but that would have been protesting too much. "You are quite charming," Charles said, placing both his hands on the bar so that they were half lit, half in shadow.

"When did you arrive?" I asked, frantic for small talk.

"Oh, just yesterday. I'm staying at the same hotel as you this go around. Did you receive the email invitation to the dinner tonight?"

"I did."

"You'll join us?"

"Yes."

"Did you bring that black lace dress of yours?"

"No-no. I don't think I packed it."

"Well, wear something like that," he banged his fist against the bar. "Can we have another round please?" I finished my beer quickly and took down my hair from atop my head. "You've done exactly what I need," he said sipping the last slop from his glass.

I was starting to feel nauseous again, unsure if it was from the pint or that I lost more than I gained in this exchange. Charles seemed to doubt my capabilities as more than a woman. But, maybe I was just being overly dramatic and sensitive.

I tried to excuse myself to go back to the hotel. "I have to rest up before dinner. Thank you for the drink."

"So soon? I want to hear more about what you're working on and where we go from here. I think you need to advance a little…" I stood up, hooked one leg onto a rung of the bar stool to prevent myself from falling over.

"I'm sorry, I'm not feeling super well at the moment."

"Go ahead. I will take care of everything."

I could feel the bartender watching me leave and heard Charles whisper something in agreement. I wanted to walk a little to shake off the interaction. The evening had surprisingly turned warm. I walked past the hotel entrance and kept going for a couple of blocks before turning around. It was getting late and the streets were crowded as people left work.

When I got back to the room, the door was ajar. I peered in. Gretchen was still sleeping, but now wearing her slides on top of the ugly patterned bed. It was obvious that she'd gotten up tried to go about the evening and then crashed.

I thought about what she'd told me about that time she'd met Christopher for an illicit rendezvous in London in their early days. How they'd stayed at this very hotel. She'd kept this story from me until she couldn't any longer, because I needed the proper exposition to analyze another of his egregious actions. Omission was nothing to friendly transparency.

I climbed in next to Gretchen. I thought of how harsh I'd been when I heard that story about Christopher. How I thought I'd never do something like that, how much better I was. I tried to get as close as I could without waking her. The pillow was wet. I thought of that line from the movie she loved. "You smell of sweat and tears," or something like that.

Some days Gretchen liked those kinds of films. Other days, she'd say:

"I've never seen that movie, just googled its subtitled stills."

"I'm ordering eggs," Gretchen said, waking me up with the announcement.

"Whatever you want," I rolled over. "Wait, what time is it?"

"Chill, you have an hour."

"What time is it?"

"It's eight pm. Hand me the phone." She placed the order as a rush. "I'm assuming you'll want something before you go."

I got up and went to the bathroom. Gretchen went over to the window and parted the curtains. "I forget how strange this town is."

"What do you mean?" I walked out drying my hands on the white trim of a blue towel.

"London is pretty weird. It's quiet and—"

"We are on Sloan Square," I reminded her this wasn't London, but an elitist sampling.

The eggs arrived, interrupting the conversation. "You should brush your hair," Gretchen said between bites.

As I was trying to spear a tomato, my phone rang. Jack showed on the screen. Gretchen urged me to take it.

"Hi."

"Hey, how's it going out there?"

"It's fine. I am on my way to the dinner soon. How's your day?"

"Going well, 'cept I just received word it will be a late night, and I have to go back to Munich, I think. I'll be home when you get back though."

"I'm sorry." I wanted to tell him about the envelope and everything else, but Gretchen was listening intently. "Well, I'll try to give you a call a little later."

"It's cool. I just wanted to…"

"Happy you did, love you." I cut him off.

"Love you."

Gretchen reached over my lap to stick her fork in the red stewed blob on my plate. "You know, you didn't keep that short because I'm here."

"What do you mean?"

"I can almost hear the voice inside your head telling you that the reason you aren't going to get into anything with him is because I'm here. You know, like I know, that I'm not the reason."

"It's a private—"

"Okay." She picked up her dish and walked out the door.

I sat there on the bed staring out the window into the night. Five, maybe ten minutes passed and then there was a knock on the door. I got up and opened it. Gretchen stood in the doorway. She leaned into the frame, one arm outstretched to the ceiling, the other balancing an empty porcelain plate. "Did you call him back?"

"No," I said, swallowing a piece of tomato. "I will, when I'm ready to tell him I'm leaving him."

* * *

There is a line from the Belgian artist Michel Seuphor as the epigraph of Lispector's "Agua Viva," it reads,

"There must be a kind of painting totally free of the dependence on the figure—or object—which, like music, illustrates nothing, tells no story, and launches no myth. Such painting would simply evoke the incommunicable kingdoms of the spirit, where dream becomes thought, where line becomes existence."

(Michel) Seuphor was a pseudonym used by a Belgian painter named Fernand Berckelaers. It is an anagram of Orpheus, son of Calliope, the muse of epic poetry.

As Seuphor explains, abstraction can exist on the written page as it does in images.

This literal interpretation is in the space and intertextuality, seeing the book from high above, like a plane surveying crop circles below, rows of space alternating with arrangements of letters. A reverse telescopic view like photographs of Robert Smithson's Spiral Jetty, 1970 in Utah. As a picture its three inches not 1500 feet of basalt rock and salt crystals.

Here, as on this very page, the stakes are distorted.

* * *

The streets were still and quiet along the square. There was no one out, save for a man in a suit, head down barreling the other way. He acknowledged me with a shake of his umbrella and carried on, likely to his partner and kids. Trying to not think of Jack, I revisited the drama of the girls. I thought about how Charles would certainly, I was sure, notice how the others didn't take to me.

I found this upsetting, worried he wouldn't realize how standard it was, how historic and cliche and boring.

And still, I wanted their approval.

I looked around at the tidy rooftops just beginning to go all dark. The last time I'd been on that very street at a similar hour was when I had just started my internship. How young and how certain.

"Mathilde!" It was Charles's voice. I stopped and turned around. "Hold up a moment. It's so early, where are you off to? Come back to the hotel. Have a drink. I'm worried about you." He wasn't the least bit concerned about me.

"I'm fine, Charles."

"Truly?"

"Yes, truly."

"Come, Mathilde," he took my hand. I felt myself tense up. "I'm sorry about the other girls." His candor in recognizing the gang mentality calmed me until I wondered if candor was still called candor when there's an end game. "Come," he led me back to the hotel steps away. We took the elevator upstairs.

"What do you mean?" I asked again and he didn't answer or say anything at all until we were somehow in his room.

"I get it, you're a shy girl." He said as if he was helping me do what I wanted to, but couldn't. I shook my head and then he started kissing me even as I turned my face away. He took my hands and directed them to touch him in a rhythmic assault.

He kept placing my hands on him. He pulled me over to the bed and stood at the edge and held me sitting upright on the side, maneuvering my mouth just across from his hard sex. And I looked up at him with wide eyes, unable to move. He was very tall. And he looked down at me with that same fixed pleased, proud expression from earlier at the bar.

He pulled my hair back, which made a shiver, held it up away from my face with one hand, while he undid his pants with the other. He pushed my head down to music heard only in his head.

The next time he spoke he said, "I'll go ahead to the restaurant. You can wash up in the bathroom." He walked out letting the door shut behind him.

The girls were waiting.

* * *

Endless text messages, transcribed voicemails, tweets (subtweets!), photo captions, and more text.

Text as reproduction, screenshot sent to twenty of your closest friends. One gets half the conversation, another the whole thing. Delete that one line for the third.

Forward the email for analysis, but cut out the time stamp and maybe that part where you sound kind of manic.

What does that bit on Whats App mean where it says "end to end encryption?"

All conversation is encrypted.

There's the book by Marguerite Duras called The Ravishing of Lol Stein. *This is the English title. The original French includes the first letter of Ms. Stein's middle name, "V."*

Who knows why. It can't be read in the same way in English anymore anyways. All you see is the "Laugh Out Loud."

LOL V

Three letters in the title of a text. That alone is confusing. What bits make up the message? One one, two, two, one, one, one. In an age of hybridity why is the transmission binary?

* * *

I started gathering my things all along the top of the sink: two black shiny compacts, a brush, a metal tube and a milky glass plastic bottle. Gretchen's creams were open and exploded. I took a towel from the rod below and wiped away the hardened nodules. She was watching me through the sliver of door hinge. I became more and more frantic, scrubbing and then folding and refolding the cloth. After the third round, she got up and came in, closing the door all the way behind her. She put her back up against it and her hands down at her sides as if she dare not come any closer, and I dare not try to get out.

"It will be okay, Tilly. It's only been like seventy two hours. You need distance."

Had it only been three days? It felt like a season of toxic strive.

Gretchen left the room.

I sank to the floor holding the phone to my chest. I pressed his name again and waited for the bleat, and then hung up.

There was a knock on the door five minutes later.

"Who is it?" I asked.

"Who do you think?"

I opened the door.

It was unseasonably hot and bright uptown. All seven floors of the office building were empty, all our colleagues having gone outside to enjoy the air. We found the heat uncomfortable, worse for all the barely clothed unkempt people. The streets were filled with them and there was odor in the air. It was midday, too hot to eat at our usual square table. We stayed in the office. Alice was busy cleaning out Mathilde's desk anyway.

"Can you believe she did that?"

"What an idiot."

"You have to try to make that mistake."

"She sent not one, but four works to the wrong address."

"Four."

"To some organic farm in Cologne."

"Apparently she also gave his secretary a fake email."

"Charles was so fucking mad."

"She's lucky they were able to get them back."

"Not lucky enough to still have her job."

"It's so much better here without her."

Mathilde

November 2015, Undecided

Gretchen and I walked together to the train station. She was shuffling along in her crushed back loafers as I was rolling my luggage behind me. Her hair was pulled into a low loop at the nape of her neck, nearly hidden in the hooded sweatshirt. We must have seemed a trippy pair, one brunette, one blonde, same height, four legs, making a funny clipetty-clop through the Underground.

"I have to leave you here," Gretchen said in front of a row of turnstiles. "But, I'll see you in New York very soon."

She hugged me quickly, then pushed through the plastic doors without saying anything else. I waved at her as she walked down the stairs towards the airport shuttle. The train time table was twirling its squares, a spin of digits. When they stopped, each landed on a letter or number, spelling out destinations and times. I had fifteen minutes before my departure. The gate was close by, so I decided to stop at the nearest kiosk.

An announcement came over the system calling for everyone to mind their belongings. I felt in my handbag for my phone and passport. The same voice said that the Eurostar would be leaving from Track One. I typed in the information to make sure there was a car to meet me at the Paris station and take me to my final stop.

Eleven rue d'Alsace. Seven Eight One Zero Zero. She'd been twenty four when I was born, it took that plus five years to meet her here.

Alone, but suddenly with a story. No longer unmoored. Held down, because I refused to go back somewhere.

ABOUT THE AUTHOR

Stephanie LaCava is a writer based in New York City. Her work has appeared in *Harper's Magazine*, *Artforum*, *Texte zur Kunst*, the *New York Review of Books*, *Interview*, and *Vogue* where she worked for five years.